ROCKING PLAYER

VICTORIA PINDER

D1524983

Love in a Book

Rocking Player

Copyright©2020

This book is a work of fiction. The names, characters, places and incidents are the product of the author's imagination or are used fictitiously. Any resemble to actual events, business establishments, locales, or persons, living or dead, is entirely coincidental.

All rights reserved. No part of this publication may be reproduced, stored in a retrieval system, or transmitted in any form or by any means (electronic, mechanical, photocopying, recording, or otherwise) without prior written permission of both the copyright owner and the publisher. The only exception is brief quotations in printed reviews.

The scanning, uploading, and distribution of this book via the Internet or via any other means without the permission of the publisher is illegal and punishable by law. Please purchase only authorized electronic editions and do not participate in or encourage electronic piracy of copyrighted materials.

Your support of author's rights is appreciated.

Published in the United States of America.

Copyright © 2020 Victoria Pinder Love in a Book

All rights reserved.

This book is dedicated to the city of Boston where I grew up. I learned about the four seasons with sports and especially the importance of baseball when I learned to walk and talk. Red Sox nation, forever. And sure I wore a Miami Marlins outfit to my sister's wedding in Boston to bug her but that was just in fun. And now that I'm living in Pittsburgh, I have to say my neighbors might love their teams like how Bostonians love ours. Talking about baseball in this book was like returning home in some way though I tried to keep the team fictional. (You will never catch me in a Yankee's hat though I LOVE visiting NYC.)

Series information

Please check out the entire **Steel Series**

Rocking Player

Ruthless Financier

Wicked Cowboy

Powerful Prince

Cocky M.D.

Scottish Seducer

Legendary Rock Star

Cinder of Ashes

Playing for Keeps (Fierce Fighter)

Treasured (Look for announcement soon)

Victoria Pinder wants to hear from you! If you're on social media, please friend her.

Join Victoria's Bold and Foxy Street Team

You can also find her here:

Sign up for her newsletter and get a FREE novella.

Follow on Facebook

Follow on Twitter

Chapter 1

Georgiana

Life wasn't like it was in the movies.

I tugged my brown hair into a ponytail, reminding myself that as a single mom, I had zero interest in dating. My son, Jeremy, was all that mattered since the day I had him.

Well, Jeremy and peace. I liked my life orderly and calm.

Once in a while, like today, I wondered what my vacation romance, the one that had transformed me into sudden mom, might react if I ever saw him again to tell him about his son. No other man since Michael had ever made me forget myself.

I was about to go to a professional baseball

game. Jeremy had begged me to take him. My son was all about the cards and getting better at catching for his little league team.

My dad, not my mom, had taken me to one baseball game as a girl, though I'm sure I'd talked his ear off about my paintbrushes I'd loved.

Nothing stirred. Not even a leaf on a tree blew outside the windows on our cul-de-sac. Silence in the house wasn't good, though at six years old, he was now old enough that maybe the quiet was okay, and it didn't mean disaster was brewing. My big ears usually heard everything, and quiet ricocheted through my spine. Time to stop my wandering thoughts. Old habits kicked in and I moved faster to get ready to take him to the game today. I checked myself in the mirror of my en suite bathroom in my two-story home. Jeans that weren't "mom jeans" and actually flattered me had been a gift from my sister, Ridley, after I'd cooked dinner for her last week. My high cheekbones were bare as blush seemed silly for a game.

I never wore makeup anymore, but all my sisters had agreed I needed to stop hiding. I wasn't, but I just wasn't interested in anyone, not since Michael and that dream vacation.

Jeremy was at his desk by the window overlooking our quiet street reading his baseball cards like he'd one day like to be stamped on one of them.

I backed out of his room and closed my eyes in the small hall next to the linen closet. Today I imagined Michael close and his kiss still made me tingle. *Sounds so stupid when I think it, but it's true.* I opened my eyes. After Michael, no other guy had made me feel anything. And I had our boy who looked like him with those blue eyes and squared chin, so I knew whatever it was between us had happened.

Time to finish and get to the day game on time. Now. Jeans were heavy, so I paired it with a plain white t-shirt as baseball games were hot just sitting in the sun. At least, I would imagine so, because I didn't remember many details from the one time as a girl with my dad.

Jeremy had begged and I'd do anything for my son. Unlike my mother, who often hid away as a wallflower, never taking me anywhere except the grocery store where I'd been the one to fill the cart with the list as she'd claim some headache and need to sit down, I made time to take Jeremy where he wanted.

Another of my five sisters, Indigo, had sent the baseball tickets from her job, so this wish of his wasn't costing anything but time and lunch. Indigo had joked I needed to check out the single dads in the stands, not that I'd ever try.

Once I'd tasted perfection, no other man had ever come close.

I lathered the sunblock on myself, quickly fixed the fine strays of my hair in the ponytail then checked my traffic apps for the quickest, safest route.

This was the nicest looking I got. No makeup, no jewelry. Single mom and now raising my son in the same home where I'd been raised with my five little sisters and countless cousins who'd come to stay with us, including Phoenix Steel, the rock star, who was the closest thing I had to a friend these days.

I heard my son rumbling ·and pacing, so I rushed out of my bedroom and grabbed the car keys on my dresser. My phone rang. Stephanie, my sister, who had defied our sisterly bond to never marry, now lived with her husband-to-be. I answered fast and said, "I can't believe you're living in London now."

She laughed. "Georgiana, you have to take Jeremy and fly over. We have room in our flat."

The cheer in her voice couldn't be replicated. I'd never have that, not that I needed more. Being a mom was great and, once in a while, we had wonderful calm in the house. I laughed as I said, "You already sound European. I'll miss seeing you, but I'm so happy for you."

"Remember that trip the six of us all took to New York?" She asked.

I cringed at the memory. Stephanie and Indigo had spent half an hour talking me off a bench in Central Park as I was overwhelmed with all the people moving.

In Pittsburgh, I loved the windy back roads with no traffic to navigate over Manhattan and being lost in a sea of people. "Yeah?"

"London's even worse, which is why we're getting a house in the country. When you come for the wedding, we can all stay together."

Go to London. I worked at a superstore filling online orders. My savings from the inheritance had all gone to Jeremy. Phoenix, my sisters, and a few cousins all pooled together funds for me when I had to quit my financial job after giving birth, but that money was for Jeremy's college and his future.

And, the superstore had insurance, which was good, as Jeremy was a kid and might need medical care. Doctor bills could wipe out every dime faster than a recession.

"I know none of us wanted to marry. I was the different one, but being in love is a good thing."

Our mom had always tried to hide herself as the eternal wallflower who hated going outside, and once our father had died, she'd withered away like she needed the oxygen only our father provided. I'd not be that crazy.

"I want love...for Jeremy."

I knew she wanted the best for me, and she'd hug me like that might make me change my mind as she said, "I love you, Sis."

My son called up the stairs, "Mom, are you ready?"

This was his day. I told Stephanie that I had to go and rushed down the stairs. I'd call my sister back later.

He was dressed and pacing. Our shoe shelf was near the door. I grabbed my sneakers, the one extravagance I'd bought myself this year, and headed to our Rav 4 parked in our garage.

We were fine. I was lucky that my inheritance had been enough to fund Jeremy's college, and being a single mom with my part-time gig meant I could be there for my boy and keep insurance.

I didn't need to be my sisters, who all had fancy careers to complete their lives.

And I absolutely didn't need a man. Jeremy was enough. So I needed to stop living in my head already. I checked his seat belt and closed his door.

Then, I took the driver's seat and said to him, "I don't know anything about baseball. You're going to have to explain everything."

He rolled his blue eyes. He wore his little league cap that read "Sea Horse" and a Pirates jersey. "I play shortstop, and you come to all my games."

In seven years, he'd be a teenager and my son would do worse than give me that look of his that read "annoyed". I cringed as I imagined him as a rebellious teenager. His father had been wild and fun. I tapped the steering wheel as we headed the few miles into the city with the skyscraper horizon surrounded by the rivers to park at the stadium for the game.

Other families were walking through the parking lot, then heading inside, laughing and joking, and mentioning the hot dogs. The game had been a good idea.

I held my son's hand. "Okay, we need to find these seats and you'll have to explain the players and whose good or not and why."

He pointed to the overhead sign and said the team names. "Today the Pirates play the Sooners. One of my favorite players will be here."

"That sounds awesome." When I played completely dumb and let him explain, I helped his self-esteem, so I asked, "And the Pirates are from here?"

He gave me a pointed look like my father would have made at me if I'd ever shown disloyalty to my hometown team. "Yeah, and the Sooners are from Tulsa."

Well, that made sense. I'd never been to Oklahoma, but of course they'd be the Sooners. I used to like history, so I knew that name was the settlers' moniker for going the night before the race to claim land and camping out near the flag sites before the race had started. Once racers had closed in, they'd put their flags up and had pretended they'd won.

I read on our ticket that we were in section 9, which Indigo, my sister, said was the closest tickets she could get last minute. It was right next to the Sooners' dugout. But it was fine. I maneuvered us around the crowd to find the seats.

"And they play the same way you do?"

Jeremy, with his short brown hair and long sides and bangs in some strange style, said, "They're better. I can't catch the ball that good. Can we get a hot dog?"

"Sure," I said and noticed his nose was red from the sun already. My shoulders slumped. I should get him a hat for the sun. Today he could study the pros. At home, I had nothing more to help. Jeremy had wanted someone to toss the ball around with, but I couldn't. I'd tried, but he'd given up on my catching and tossing skills once he'd realized they were worse than his.

I needed to figure out how to help him and who to ask. I walked toward the stand outside our numbered section and ordered a couple of hot dogs, sodas, and popcorn.

He carried his food and we filed in. Indigo had been right. We could smell the fresh grass. Hopefully, Jeremy saw whoever his favorite was from our vantage point.

Jeremy slipped into his seat and hugged the popcorn as he said, "Mom, these are great seats. We can see the dugout."

I laughed and settled in, putting my drink in the seat holder. "I only get you the best, kid. You know that."

"Thanks, Mom," he said as the seats around us filled in.

I checked my phone, which was empty of messages, but that was fine. No sisters or cousins in crisis that needed my ear today, as the second mom of the entire Steel clan. My first real responsibility in the world was next to me. I put it away and smelled the fresh popcorn and beer and listened to people around me mentioning some player named

"Irons" with some amazing batting average as the one the Pirates needed to fear.

Everyone was smiling, including Jeremy, who looked enraptured with the field.

I tapped his side and said, "Okay, tell me what's going on."

The team in the dugout beside us started coming out.

Jeremy said, "That's Rodriguez. He's the pitcher for the Sooners."

We could see them lining up to go on the field and I said without looking, "I see."

The next man on the huge Jumbotron had that chiseled chin I'd never forget. Jeremy had inherited it.

"That's Michael Irons," Jeremy added the name I'd wondered about for years.

Adrenaline coursed through me as I glanced toward the field and saw the player in question.

The player who'd rocked my world.

Irons spit out whatever was in his mouth and waved to the crowd as I asked with an almost breathless voice, "Who?"

"He's the shortstop and has the best batting average in the league."

Shortstop. MVP. Weekend fling. Father of my son. My heart trembled,

I grabbed my soda from its holder and said, "Jeremy, we need to go."

His gaze narrowed, and he didn't move. "What's going on?"

"Get up."

I pushed at him. If he saw me, I'd find out in a second if he even remembered our moment. I'd had my memories and his son. We needed to leave. Now.

He didn't move from his seat. "Mom, we just got here."

My skin had chills as I grabbed my son's arm. "I'll explain later. Please run."

He stood, shook his head at me, and put his hands in his pockets. "Mom, we're here, and you promised to take me to a game. Your phone didn't ring, so nothing happened to anyone."

A warmness stirred in my belly as someone came behind me, probably for their seats next to us as I tugged my son and said, "I'll get better tickets tomorrow."

"Mom, turn around," Jeremy said as his eyes widened.

My skin had goosebumps it hadn't had in a long time. "Why?"

He pointed and said like he couldn't quite breathe, "It's Michael Irons, the shortstop."

I turned around and stared into the stormy blue eyes of Michael, Jeremy's father.

"I never thought I'd see you again."

I'd stopped looking for any signs of my vacation romance years ago.

I never should have stopped. His hand wrung the hat he held in his hands as he asked, "Georgiana? I never got your last name?"

That was it?

I'd played this scenario over a thousand times in my head, but I stilled and just said, "Michael, hi."

Jeremy now took my hand. "Mom, do you know Michael?"

Not once had I imagined the muscular man in my bed had been a baseball player. I probably should have guessed he was an athlete, as he was still all muscles, but somehow even sexier than my memory.

Maybe it was the skintight pants.

My face felt hot as I said, "No. I mean, yes. Kind of. We met years ago, on vacation, before I had you."

Michael stared at Jeremy and then at me. He widened his stance. He knew.

He saw a mini version of himself, square jaw,

blue eyes, pointed nose. "You checked out of the hotel early."

My entire body felt tight, like I was going to rocket my own flight out of here from the energy in my veins. "I...My father died. Then my mom soon after. I was a mess and my life was in turmoil for a while."

He took my hand in his. "You didn't leave a way to find you."

"Michael Irons!" Jeremy said fast. "You've got the best batting average and record of catches in the league."

Of course. The one thing our son craved to be better at was the one thing his father was clearly good at. He took out his phone from his back pocket and shoved it in my face as the stadium-filled crowd around us became clearer.

Michael quickly said, "Look, give me your address and phone number. I have to work, but after the game, we need to talk. Clearly."

Talk. Right. Of course. I'd played out finding him and telling him about his son for years now, but it generally was me in a sexy dress strutting over to him and then he'd kissed me in my dreams of this moment. Now, real-life was different, and my fingers trembled.

Still, I typed down my information and handed

him back his phone as Michael asked, "Can we stay at the game, Mom?"

Jeremy's lips thinned.

I wish I knew what he thought, but I asked with my head down, "How long do games last?"

Michael answered in a deep voice that had once made me swoon, "A few hours usually, and I'd like us all to go out to dinner after."

Jeremy's bounce and jumping beside me meant he wanted to. I had no argument. My son had wanted to know his father. Searching out who he was online had been impossible when I'd been so busy looking up cures for my mom that never panned out. And when she'd died, I'd been in my third trimester, more worried about what to do to prepare for a baby than anything else.

I nodded at Jeremy and wished things had been different as I said, "Then we'll stay."

Michael put his Sooners cap back on. "I'll see you both right after we win."

"Boo." The red-headed, overweight man behind us screamed. He had the Pirates logo painted on his cheeks.

I slumped onto the bench and Michael strutted away with that hard, muscular ass I'd once squeezed. He spoke with someone on the team and then they both stared at us.

My jitters were still inside me as I stabbed the ice with my straw in my soda.

Another man, skinnier, wearing a uniform like Michael but much younger than him, ran toward us as the team went onto the field to play. "The team wants to offer the two of you family seats."

I grabbed Jeremy's arm like someone might steal him from me. Family with Michael sounded permanent.

I trembled a little and squared my jaw when I said, "We're fine here."

The young man then backed away and said, "Well, at the top of the ninth, I'll come to find you both."

"Great," I said and then slumped into my seat.

Jeremy stood and the second I heard the national anthem, I jumped up.

At the end of the singing, and someone in a wheelchair tossing a ceremonial pitch, we took our seats and the game began.

My son asked, "Mom, how do you know Michael Irons?"

Clearly, I was a liar. And a bad one. Maybe I should have at least looked at his baseball cards once or twice, but that wasn't my interest. I bet I probably had seen his face in passing, but I'd never connected the dots. I'd been more into ensuring

Jeremy had what he needed for school, clothes, and ate to stay healthy.

A head rush came from having to explain everything to a six-year-old and then to a sexy grown man right after.

I slumped my head down and didn't care who was hitting what ball on the field and said to Jeremy, "I... we met at a hotel. I didn't know he was a professional baseball player."

Jeremy sounded like my father when he asked, "Where was this hotel?"

I'd been a financial analyst when I'd met Michael. I had gone on an adults-only vacation with some friends who I was no longer close to.

"The Bahamas. The resort was nice."

Jeremy's lips thinned and his bright blue eyes didn't blink. "And you bumped into Michael then?"

"I'd been swimming in the pool when he came and joined me."

Life had been so easy then. He'd joined me, bought me a drink, and whispered naughty ideas in my ear. My face heated when I remembered how many times his cock had made me writhe in pleasure. I hadn't wanted anyone else since.

"Jeremy, remember when you asked me who your father was, and I told you I didn't know?"

His eyebrows shot up. "Yeah."

I'd read books about this on the off chance the situation arose on how to explain why I was a single mom.

"I didn't know what happened to Michael or his last name. I thought it was better to assume I'd... we'd never see him again."

After a long pause, Jeremy's face brightened and said, "Michael Irons is my father?"

I lowered my voice. "Don't say that out loud."

His face lit up as if he just saw the gifts under the tree. "Maybe he can teach me to be a better shortstop like him."

Maybe. He might be married, have children of his own, a girlfriend. And I didn't exactly believe I'd ever marry. What if I transitioned into my mother, who'd accepted whatever my father had said without her own opinion?

A shadow came over me and there wasn't a cloud in the sky as I said, "We can't assume he'll even want to see us again."

"Why not? He wants to see us."

Out of the mouth of babes. Just because his sperm found my egg once, it did not mean he wanted a lifetime commitment. And I wasn't exactly good wife material.

"Because he doesn't know about us."

Jeremy shrugged and ate some of his popcorn. "This game is better than I dreamed, Mom."

Or the worst day of my life.

I closed my eyes and wished I'd have looked up more about my son's interest in professional baseball, figured out Michael's last name, and called the hotel for Michael's name, or any number of crazy things I could have done but didn't.

"That's good for one of us."

When Michael walked away from us, I'd be left to pick up the pieces of my son's broken heart. I wasn't sure how I'd handle it, but I had no choice. I needed to see him, too.

How could I ever imagine the man who rocked my world years ago would turn out to be a baseball player? All I remembered was sitting at a pool bar where he whispered naughty things in my ear and convinced me to go to his room with him.

Chapter 2

Michael

A fucking son. One that looked exactly like my dad, with those bright blue eyes that captured my attention. This was like a dream, or nightmare, that roared to life in my work hours.

I was absolutely sure and didn't need to be told I had a son. That weekend in the Bahamas after my rookie year had been unforgettable because of Georgie.

Her kiss had left me reeling and no one else's tasted right. And, from my quick view, Georgie's body was almost the same, though her backside was rounder with sexier curves than I remembered.

Big Michael was already ready for her now that I'd found her again.

My mind spun. This wasn't fucking good.

I'd looked at her hands for a ring. I was clearly crazy, but my body was tense and hard when I'd made it back to the dugout, as I'd wanted to stake my claim.

And every lull in the game had had me glancing over to the brunette and her...*our* son in a fucking Pirates hat. I was sure of it.

A ball flew past me.

Damn, I needed to get my head straight. I missed a routine grounder.

As we left the first inning, the second baseman, Rogers, patted me on my back and asked, "So you have a family?"

I wasn't the only one seeing my family's face stamped on that boy.

I tugged at my jersey collar and said, "Apparently, her parents died, and that's why she went AWOL on me seven years ago."

Rogers knew I'd spent the second year on the road scanning the crowds for Georgie to show up. And the third year. And a bit of the fourth. He didn't know how I rejected every other woman's offer because no one else smelled or tasted right after being with Georgie.

She'd never showed, until now.

Rogers asked, "And she showed up at your game with your son?"

"Clearly." I wrapped my hands for batting lineup.

Rogers did the same. "Girls like her will always exist. After the game, pay her off and be done with her. Right now, we need your head in the game."

No. Even in the hotel, Georgie had been…sweet and memorable. I'd taken out her picture on my phone we'd taken together the day we met at the pool and wished I'd find her again before the start of every game, including now. Praying for her was part of my warm-up routine, but now that prayer was answered.

I squared my shoulders as my turn was coming up but only said, "I play to win."

I grabbed my bat and tested it as I made my way to the plate. I stepped on the white plate to signal I was ready. I refused to glance anywhere except into the pitcher's brown eyes.

The catcher behind me smacked his gums and said, "So Michael, you were hiding that one away good."

A ball flew past my head over a hundred miles per hour.

I spit and talked back in the same tone. "I wore your mother out last night."

He laughed. "Yet, it's your son wearing a Pirate's jersey there, buddy."

Fire burst through my veins.

At the crack of the bat, I said, "Take that, fuckers," and ran.

I made it to third and stopped as I knew I couldn't barrel my way into home on time.

Georgie and her boy were a direct sight in my line of vision now. The hot blazing sun made her seem heaven-sent to me, and my son was like an added bonus.

His existence meant she'd never forgotten me. And hopefully meant she'd be open to more, because I needed her body. Seven years of pent up energy with only her picture for inspiration had been excruciating.

Soon, Rogers hit the ball, and I made it home on his single.

The crowd jeered. Pirates' fans were clearly passionate. I wished my own team had been that enthusiastic about my skills during the contract negotiations. As I made it back to my dugout, I saw some fans talking smack to Georgie in the field.

She held her son closer as Rodriguez asked me,

"Is she why you're ditching us at the end of the season?"

I ignored my friend and walked closer to see what was going on.

Fans were screaming at Georgie for bringing the Pirates bad luck as I said, "I'm following the Benjamins. It's what brought me here and my agent is combing through all offers. It has nothing to do with her."

If the Sooners had shown me loyalty with their offer, I'd have stayed. I liked my team.

However, I walked into the crowd again as he asked behind me, "You joining these fuck-heads because your girl is here?"

Rodriquez didn't need an answer. I signaled Aaron, the water and errand boy of the team, to join me.

I jumped up to where she was, and she made sweaty stands somehow smell like summer. "Georgie?"

"Yeah?" She asked and clutched her son with her face white and tight, like she expected a bomb to go off.

I snapped at Aaron to help me out again and said, "Can you get to the family seating area already so you're both safe?"

Georgie looked around and then nodded. "On our way."

I couldn't walk with her. I rejoined my team, but I saw Aaron walking her to the family seats, where no one else would ever hit her off the back of the head or scream in her face.

Georgie had no idea, but she'd been the only girl I'd dreamed about and the last person in my pathetic bed for years now, and that was pretty telling as I traveled around the country for a living. Rodriguez had married, divorced, and married another while I'd been in fucking limbo waiting for Georgie.

The next inning went better.

I caught every ball and light had returned to my step.

This time, I followed all my usual routines and when I went up to plate, I didn't hear a word of the pitcher's smack talk. I hit the ball like it was a softball, and it made it over the wall.

The crowd jeered as the announcer said, "Homerun."

"That was awesome." Rogers dug his cleats into the field as I neared the dugout.

I detoured to go to the family area as I said fast, "My lucky charm is here."

I didn't care that the cameras heard me or that my team saw.

I returned to where she was and smelled the dewy sweetness.

The cameras were all on me, and adrenaline from the homerun was still in my veins, as I grabbed her soft sides like no time had passed.

Georgie softened and her eyelids lowered.

She still felt good in my arms as she said, "Michael!"

Her fingers twirled in my hair and I pressed against her and said, "We'll talk after."

Without thinking, I pressed my lips to hers and fireworks exploded in my veins. My memories had all been right. She was fucking perfect.

She kissed me back, her hands in my thick hair and her soft lips that set me off made me forget where I was. I'd shaved part of my skull and she massaged it in a way only Georgie had ever done.

For one second, I was transported back in time to when I'd met her in the pool. She'd not asked for my rookie autograph. She'd just been pretty in her yellow bikini that I'd found a way to get off her that very night.

As the kiss ended, the world returned to color. I remembered where I was and saw the open mouth of my father in her young son's face.

The announcer overhead said, "Michael Irons caught on the kiss cam."

I glanced at the Jumbotron. Everyone in the stadium must have seen it. My agent would call this reckless unless I claimed her as mine fast.

I winked at her and as I made it back to my dugout, I heard the announcer ask, "Will Michael be joining the Pirates next season? His son is wearing a Pirates shirt."

That would be corrected. I went where the money was. The Sooners hadn't shown up with the right dollar sign to show their desire to keep me, and I wasn't fucking waiting for them. Team loyalty was for players who wanted to stay poor and this was quite possibly my last million-dollar contract before I retired.

I guess it shouldn't matter. I had enough money to not care, except I did. I needed the money as evidence I was the best. It validated my years of hard work to perfect my game.

I refused to ever be a poor kid from the corn-fields who didn't know any better than how to lose a dime of my money.

In college, I'd studied finance. That time, combined with my skill of the game, had secured my future, for when this ended.

Truthfully, I'd never pictured my life after

leaving the field forever, except having more in the bank was better as life threw curveballs, like having a son with Georgie.

Now, I had a son to ensure his financial well-being and I didn't know his name. I would remedy that. Fast.

The last batter was up, and I watched with my team. Unless the Pirates pulled off a miracle, the game was ours.

But I still held my breath as I always did when the relief pitcher tossed the potential final ball.

The batter swung but missed.

We won. I high fived my team and then took the field to shake hands with the other team. Who honestly knew. Maybe the Pirates did have the best offer for me next year. Anything was possible, my son and my woman lived here, and I told my agent we'd look over the numbers in the range I wanted when I got back to Tulsa.

Free agenting was a blur, but for now, it didn't matter. The Sooners needed to pony up if they wanted me. I left my team, who were heading into the locker room, and motioned for the water boy to join me.

As I neared Georgie again, the air smelled like her floral scent. I'd forgotten her smell until today.

I placed my hand on her back and she jumped.

"Look, the game is over. I need you both to follow Aaron. I'll meet you as soon as I'm free."

Her big brown eyes captured my attention as she asked, "Aaron?"

Part of me wanted to grab her, rip her clothes off and make her mine right here on the field. But her son was beside her, and I wanted to meet him, too.

So I nodded and patted the water boy's back as I said, "He'll get you to the family waiting area so we can leave."

I took a step back, but she craned her neck as she glanced toward me and asked, "Where are you going?"

I winked. My veins still had energy that I needed to get under control. "Shower, change, and give some interviews. Give me ten minutes."

I turned, but she asked, "Michael?"

I smiled at her and glanced at the boy whose pinched face was exactly like my father's when I screwed up and didn't catch the ball. "We'll talk, Beautiful. It seems we have a lot of catching up to do."

A fast shower helped clear my head. The boy was mine. I'd still want a test to confirm for the lawyers and the estate, but I wasn't blind. As I left the shower, Paulie Rodriguez called from the ice machine for me to come over.

I threw some jeans on and he asked, "Who was the woman you were kissing?"

"An old friend," I said, though I fully remembered how Georgie's arms around me as I took her in every direction felt like. It was like sex with her branded me because no other woman's lips or body captured my attention.

The few second chance smoke kisses planted on me left me reeling, like I'd betrayed Georgie, so I never pursued women. Finally, I knew Georgie's address and phone number. She was back in my life and I wasn't giving her up.

I had a shot at reclaiming those moments.

Paulie gave me a wolfish smile. "You called her your lucky charm. How have we never seen her before when you've had a stellar career?"

"And no signs of stopping," I answered fast.

I'd not be swayed with team friendships for going after the big money contract when the Sooners hadn't shown that to me. This was my time.

His gaze narrowed as he asked, "Right, so who is she?"

I took out my phone and showed him my

sacred picture of us at the moment we'd met at the pool. "For the past seven years, I've been carrying her picture with me on my phone. When I look at her face, I win. If I miss this routine, I lose. So, I've been seeing this picture of us for years."

The yellow bikini had caught my eye that day and when I'd succeeded in my mission of removing it, she'd branded me forever.

I grabbed one of the team hats and tucked it in my back pocket as Paulie asked, "And the boy?"

Mine, but who knows what would happen next right now.

I put my phone back and waved to him. "Stay tuned. Look, I got to go."

Reporters caught me. I talked about having a good game and how I was open to all offers with the right amount of perks.

One reporter asked about Georgie and the boy in the Pirates shirt.

I pressed my hand to my heart and said, "I thought I lost the love of my life. Wish me luck in having a second chance with her."

I avoided mentioning my son. If they asked me about him, I didn't want to admit I had no idea about his name or any details.

"You're too good to pass up," the female reporter said, looking me up and down.

Good. I avoided the topic and sauntered up the aisle. My stomach had butterflies like I was nervous, as made my way toward the lot where families reunited.

Maybe I was on overdrive. I'd finally found her again and now I had a few hours to be near her.

My wishes were about to come true as I opened the door.

There was Georgie. Her brown hair still in a ponytail, plain white shirt that hid her beautiful orbs and sexier hips that I could hold onto when I rammed myself into her.

And yes, that was going to happen.

I'd have her again. That wasn't destiny or fate or any such bullshit. Having her again was my future, and I didn't need a crystal ball to know that.

She had her arms crossed as Rogers stopped me from going to her side.

I paused as my teammate said, "You just made it sound like you're in love."

I needed her, but the last thing I needed was locker room gossip, so I shrugged, "It's what the media likes, and who knows, maybe it will help increase the offers and make me look more stable."

"A shark as always," Rogers said and headed back into the stadium.

I finally made it to the top of the walkway and

saw how she clutched the boy's hand. I took off his Pirates hat and put a Sooners hat on his head.

He smiled at me as his mother said, "I've been googling your life for the past few hours."

If I'd known her full name years ago, we'd not be here now because I'd have found her. I placed my hand on her back to direct her toward the player's parking lot so we might get out of there.

She didn't stop me as I said, "Don't believe everything you read."

She paused near the door and covered her son's ears as she asked, "So you didn't get caught with a...prostitute...in LA?"

My entire body froze as that moment replayed in my mind. She'd been a gift from Rogers that I'd never wanted.

"There is more to that story."

Her face was red as she asked, "How?"

Four years ago, Rogers had called my newfound celibacy a dry spell. I'd not wanted to date since Georgie, but he'd been trying to help me out and resorted to hiring some woman who then had her friend snap a picture of us and got it in the news. I'd been escorting her out while assuring her that she'd keep the money my friend had paid. Then we'd walked right into a group of reporters and she'd given interviews without me.

I squared my shoulders now and said to the one person this mattered to. "I didn't touch her except to get her out of the hotel room, fast."

"Hmm," Georgie said, with her arms crossed.

I reached for the door. "We'll talk more when we're out of here."

She let her son's ears go. "Where should we meet you?"

"What are you talking about?" I asked and pointed out to the lot.

She pointed backward and jangled her keys. "We'll get in our car and meet you at a restaurant."

I held the door for her. "We'll send for your car or I'll drop you off later." The pair of them walked with me to my silver Audi R8 Spyder and I opened my passenger seat as I said, "Get in."

Her face looked like I'd just told her to eat dirt off the ground. "You don't have enough seats."

Her boy, whose name was still a mystery, tugged on her arm and stepped inside as he said, "Mom, we'll make it work."

Smart boy. He hopped into the tiny back with his surprisingly long legs. I watched as she took the seat next to mine and then I closed the door.

Once I revved the engine, I didn't ask the burning question in my mind of her last name, where she'd been, or my son's name.

Instead, I asked, "How old are you?"

"Six," he answered.

I glanced in the mirror as I took off. "And what's your name?"

"Jeremy," he said.

I tapped the wheel as we peeled out of the lot, and I did the math. The name I didn't recognize, but six would be about right.

"That's what I thought."

He asked, as his mother glared at me, "You did?"

I met Georgie's sidelong look as I drove them toward my hotel. It was the best place to have a private conversation, which I hoped she understood.

"Yeah, you look exactly like my dad."

Her lips were thin as she said, "He looks like you."

Was that an admission?

She'd had my son without telling me, but I just said, "Then I recognized the family resemblance."

I never thought I looked like my dad, but I wasn't about to argue as that seemed silly. Georgie's lips were tight as she locked that gaze on me like she could burn into my skin, but said nothing.

Jeremy then asked, "So you know you're my father?"

Her face went almost purple as I drove into the lot of the hotel nearby. "I need your mom to confirm that."

She glanced out the window as I pulled into valet and asked, "Why?"

I leaned closer to her. Up close, she was sweet enough to wet my lips.

I burned with the need to have her again. "Call me old fashioned, but I need to hear it with my own ears."

She reached for the door and hopped out as she said, "Fine. He's your son."

Our son followed her. We were this close to being alone. I had no idea how to seduce a woman with a child present. But Jeremy seemed like a good kid, and I needed to find out more about my son.

My dad had been hard on me, but ultimately his drilling me taught me more about baseball than anything else I'd ever done. With my own son, I wanted to be important to him, but maybe less intense, and suddenly, that thought was about to be true.

I slammed my door with more force than usual. "Then let's bring this conversation somewhere more private. Son, you pick whatever you want from room service."

For a moment, her hands went into fists at her sides, but she let them go and curled her arms around her waist instead. If she was nervous, I'd give her space until she remembered how good we were together.

Either way, now that I knew she had my son, we were bonded forever, so she might want some benefits from me, and I'd do whatever I could to get her back in bed, fast.

And I couldn't wait to see her ass again to see how having my boy had changed her.

I needed to know that, too.

Chapter 3

Georgie

I turned my phone off. Indigo, Stephanie, Ridley, Nicole, Olivia, my sisters, or Phoenix, Rocky, Ryder, Marshall, Chase, or Zuma, my cousins, who were like brothers, all called often, would ask how the game had gone and I'd have no answer. What could I say?

Ridley's tickets were a direct line to the father of my child. Turns out, he's a ballplayer.

No. I'd not say that. More questions would then follow and, honestly, it was better to avoid conversation for today when my nerves were already shot.

That decision didn't take the zap out of the air and my hair stood on its ends as I crossed the threshold to his hotel room. The last time I'd done this, we'd created Jeremy.

So I held him like he was my life preserver as the door behind us closed. Michael put the "do not disturb" sign up and locked the door.

My shoulders cringed, as we were now practically alone, and my son just let me go and asked, "Can I get a cheeseburger and fries?"

Be cool. The Michael I remembered was protective and sweet and he'd not seduce my panties off me while our son was present.

I ignored the zip in my veins and hugged my waist like I was thinking, as I asked, "That's all you want?"

"And a soda," Jeremy added as he took a seat at the table with his phone in his hand.

Michael picked up the phone to assumedly call room service.

I unhooked my arms from around my sides and said, "You already had one today."

Michael blocked the receiver so whoever was on the other line didn't hear. "He just met his father for the first time. Let him have whatever he wants."

I nodded. He ordered three cheeseburgers, one

with a salad instead of fries, which is exactly what I'd have ordered, and hung up the phone.

"I'm going to need a DNA test for the lawyers to set up a trust account for Jeremy."

I dragged my feet toward the dining table to be near my son. "That's not a problem. Look, we're not after your money."

He took a seat opposite me and asked, "Why didn't you tell me?"

The goosebumps were because his nearness made me giggly and jumpy. This wasn't still attraction, right? That wasn't going to happen.

I placed my hands on the table and said, "I didn't know your last name. I searched for you after everything with my parents but couldn't find you."

He reached out and took my hand. Definitely sparks.

"I'm in the newspapers a lot. My face has cards."

Someone knocked at the door.

He jumped up as Jeremy said, "I have your baseball card."

The tray of food came in. It must be fast service when you're a celebrity like Michael because last time I took my son on a trip, we waited an hour for room service to arrive.

This had taken five minutes or less, but Michael didn't even notice as he winked at me and said, "See, there is a picture of me in your house."

I pressed my lips together as he tipped the delivery guy, who then left without a word.

Once I heard the click of the door and Michael sat beside me, I relaxed and said, "I don't look at the cards or read newspapers. I just buy the card packs because Jeremy asks, and he's entertained in his seat."

He unwrapped his burger and Jeremy dug into his. Being near Michael rattled and made my insides bloom with awareness, but I needed to calm down. I forced my lips to curl up until I relaxed. For a few minutes, none of us said a word as we enjoyed our meal.

As the food wound down, Michael wiped his face and asked, "What is it you do, Georgie?"

My stomach twisted. Normally, whenever someone in my mom's groups complained about their job, I'd been the "at least you're not Georgie who works retail now" feel good rebuttal. I never mentioned my side business that brought in money, as it wasn't their business, and I only worked at the store for healthcare.

I wasn't looking for love or some sort of satisfaction from working when I folded my hands in front of me and said, "I raise Jeremy and work part-time filling online orders at a store."

Jeremy finished his food and pushed his plate back. "Mom quit her nice job to look after me."

Oh, no.

"My job before was boring anyhow," I said fast. No way should Jeremy ever feel guilty over that choice. I sat straighter and met Michael's clear blue eyes as I said, "Look, I'm not poor or desperate. We don't need your money to survive."

Jeremy pointed toward the living area of the room and asked, "Mom, can I go sit on the couch and play a game on my phone?"

We'd leave in a minute and get a car share back to the stadium.

For now, I ignored how my skin was still warm from Michael's nearness and just said, "Sure."

Jeremy got up and left.

Michael leaned back in his chair and asked, "How are you paying for everything you have by yourself?"

I lifted my chin.

We'd not seen each other in years, and he had no idea that I rejected every other man I met, as I asked, "How do you know I'm alone?"

His eyebrow rose and, inside, I quaked.

There was no way I wanted to lie, so my neck tensed, and I closed my eyes as I said, "Fine." For a moment, I just breathed, then I said, "My parents left enough for the six of us, but I think a few of my cousins added dollars to that inheritance."

He blinked and asked me, "Your sisters?"

He remembered that detail then. I should be flattered. Maybe part of me was. His words had sent butterflies into my chest, but I ignored that sense and said, "Yes. Though I'm the only one who chose not to work some fabulous dream job. My parents helped raise my cousins so, in many ways, they are more like brothers, and to pay tribute to my parents, they pooled their money to ensure we were all fine. I've been managing to use that to ensure Jeremy has a future."

"You still work for the day to day expenses?"

"I need healthcare for us."

"I see." He played with a piece of his short dark hair that curled. He'd done that years ago, in the same spot, as we had deep discussions on the hotel balcony. The memory of the Bahamas even had a warm breeze tonight as he asked, "And, you're happy going home alone to an empty bed?"

"Yes," I said and didn't move. I'd not be

ashamed or admit that every night I wished for his kiss. There was nothing wrong with finding home life fun.

He had his hands on the table, but leaned closer as he asked, "How? I go crazy staring at the four walls."

Writing. Painting. I enjoyed challenging myself, but he likely didn't share my interests because, honestly, I found my life more fulfilling than when I'd worked in financial services. "I do more than just work at a store."

"What else then?"

I swallowed my pride and said, "I develop websites when I'm in the mood to work."

He sat back like I'd answered his question. "So, you work from home?"

Oh, he had no idea, and I didn't bother to explain myself as he'd leave us alone soon. I shrugged my shoulder and said, "Part-time. It's nothing."

Jeremy let out an audible yawn. "Mom charges five thousand for initial set up."

Michael's eyes had a shine in them that sent heatwaves in me from that glance of his.

My son didn't even pop his head over the couch as he said, "That's decent."

"I did a few of my cousins' sites and they recommended me."

"Anyone I know?"

"Phoenix Steel, probably."

"The singer is your cousin?"

"Yes." I licked my lips and wished I didn't imagine what Michael's shaft might still do to me and if he could make me see nothing but stars when he took me.

"Good references then."

The memory was visceral sitting here with him now and discussing my family. Work. This conversation was benign. I swallowed and patted my hair like I was checking for strays and said, "If I'm going to make time for someone, I might as well charge."

He folded his hands in front of his chest, making his muscles harden under that white shirt of his. "What else do you do?'

"I read," I said and crossed my legs. At least with my child here, I'd not be tempted to do anything bad.

I was a model mom.

But he stared at my breasts like he knew what he'd done to them and awareness of him made me weak when he asked, "And?"

The heat in my face grew. I knew I'd never act

on my thoughts or feelings, but I was tempted to kiss him again and make the rest of the world black out. However, he took any calmness or peace and tossed that out the door and left me completely rattled. And I needed calmness to be a good mom. I waited till I met his gaze and pretended I was angry when I said, "I also keep house. I help my family when they need me. What is this? An inquisition?"

Michael raised his hands in the air. "I'm just curious."

The best way to change the conversation was an offense. I pressed my shoulders back and asked, "What about you?"

His gaze twinkled, and I realized he saw the black strap of my bra. I fixed it when he asked, "What about me?"

I glanced around the room and heard the distinct sound of Jeremy's snoring. "How do you spend your days in hotel rooms like this?"

Michael scooted closer and his voice rattled into my skin. "I work, I go to practice, I masturbate."

"Jeremy!" I shrieked like I'd wake him up, and my nerves were absolutely shot.

Michael shushed me and ran his finger up my bare arm that grew goosebumps from his simple touch. "He's asleep."

I jerked my chair back and stared at my Michael. The longing to wrap myself in him and only him was like a tidal wave I needed to somehow get away from. I refused to turn into my mom and needed to be calm and rational. My dreams weren't real even if I was now near the source that set me off course the rest of my life. "I should get him home."

He stood with me, but then his other arm traced mine and my body arched into him like I'd been starving. "In a few minutes. We finally get time alone."

"I don't want time alone with you," I said, but my voice was weaker.

"Why?"

"It's dangerous."

Michael Irons had been the only man in the world I'd wanted since that day we'd met. Every other man in these long years had kissed like wet fish that I ran away from fast. Maybe that was because I'd tasted paradise and hadn't forgotten perfection.

Michael laughed like he could read my thoughts, then said, "Because I said masturbate?"

Here I was in his arms, and the language was getting provocative. I tugged my arm free and retook my seat. I waited for him to do the same and said, "Yes. No. I mean, I'm not a prude, but I don't want that language anywhere near him."

He tugged on his chiseled chin. "So, you want him to learn about sex from his friends at school and not talk to you about it."

Other children, no. I closed my eyes. This wasn't something I wanted to deal with yet. And besides, I was now a full-time responsible parent and I suppose one day needed to rationally explain the birds and the bees.

"I…don't know. It's not like my parents talked to me about it." I glanced at the wall like that might focus me. "But I don't want him to get diseases, make bad choices, or die of heartbreak, because your husband died, and hurt his own children. Did yours?"

"Is that what happened to your parents?"

"Yeah."

Michael took my hand like he cared about what I said and, for that moment, I was at peace. Then he said, "My dad explained a few things, like it's healthy to tug the joystick, and I've had a lot of practice the last few years."

"Joystick. Are you serious?"

He laughed at me like I was the one who sounded ridiculous as he shrugged and said, "I liked video games as a kid, and I have my own controller."

He would consider his cock a joystick then. I rolled my eyes like I was offended when the truth was, I wasn't, but I said, "I don't need to hear this."

He asked in a lower, sexier, deep voice that made my body get all twisted up, "So you don't masturbate, Georgie?"

"No," I said, but sounded weak. I never sounded like this. It was like Michael had some power over me I couldn't describe and didn't want to. No one would believe me anyhow.

"No pretend bat scoring in your bedroom nightstand?"

"A bat…no, I don't have a vibrator."

He scooted closer in his seat. "Do you have another man in your life I need to get rid of?"

"Get rid of?" I asked and played with the collar of my V-neck t-shirt as I needed to touch something.

He pressed his hand on my thigh. "I want you, Georgie. Seven years hasn't quenched my desire for you. Time has actually enhanced it."

The same. Not even childbirth pains had stopped the memories that had brought me plea-sure for more than a few weeks. I avoided looking at him, but his hand on me just made me zap in ways I thought were dead. "I…should probably lie right now and say I do."

His hand went up my body, from my waist to my chest to my face. "Better not to lie. I can see in your eyes you want me."

I fluttered my eyes closed as I gave a weak sounding protest. "Stop this. I'm weak near you."

"So am I, Beautiful." He inched closer and I knew he stood from his seat as he said, "If I could stop wanting you, I would have, years ago."

I stood, too. He wasn't alone in this. I wanted to hate him. I'd wanted to forget him. But that hadn't happened. He'd been the only man in my bed since we'd met. I stayed in his arms as I said, "We don't know anything about each other. Whatever decision I make has consequences."

He cupped my face. "I get that."

"But you don't care," I said as my lips pressed together instead of arguing like I should. I should pick up my sleeping boy and run. I should have never been with him on that vacation either, but near Michael, all my 'shoulds' dissipated like the rules didn't apply with him.

Michael's warm breath and lips were a fraction of an inch from mine as he said, "Don't put words in my mouth. Do this instead."

He kissed me. I wanted to push him off, but my arms curled around his muscular shoulders.

I said, "Damn," between breaths.

Tomorrow was tomorrow, but for a kiss, Michael hit a homerun. He still had whatever it was about him that made my veins crave him and only him.

All he needed to do was lead.

Chapter 4

Michael

My wood was hard and needy. I hadn't been so wound up in a long time. Every other woman had tasted like I'd eaten rotten eggs if she'd kissed me, so I'd waited seven years for Georgie.

However, I'd wait more. I wasn't in a hotel anymore. The sun was starting to rise out of her north windows. I'd driven both Georgie and my boy home. As he slept and I carried him in my arms, I realized he truly was an unexpected treasure.

He was like a small little angel when he slept, though he needed a better haircut. Longer hair on the sides blocked his peripheral view to catch the ball properly.

Now that I was in Jeremy's life, I'd show him how to be a man.

Georgie's conversation last night made me think she took care of the basics but needed better health insurance. She'd been an analyst and she'd probably priced out what everything in her life cost and probabilities that hadn't. I remembered on our vacation how she'd said she had spreadsheets of math statistics to decide everything, including where she vacationed. She'd researched the hotel for crime statistics.

Last night though, she'd actively avoided planning a few things boys, in time, need to know, but I'd be here for Jeremy, too.

And to seduce Georgie into bed.

I took care of business in the basement bathroom and washed myself up and headed upstairs to her granite floor kitchen with all white cabinets and black marble counters. It was spotless, but I dug through drawers, found the waffle maker and the mixing bowl. And whipped up breakfast.

Georgie and I needed to talk. Bad. She had my son. This wasn't about lust or just tossing her on the bed and taking her anymore.

And Jeremy needed to know he had a father. I

needed to know him. My parents would want to meet him, and I needed to fucking act like a man.

Fast.

As I heard the sizzle of the machine, I found the coffee and made that, too.

However, it smelled bad and I stilled. I picked up my apps for morning delivery that I had in case any hotel coffee the team booked for us sucked. The smell of the coffee seemed off, but I waited till it finished percolating.

With one test, I knew I'd better use the app. And, coffee was ordered.

Jeremy came downstairs, and I silently made him a plate. He stared at me like I was some wonder as I held up the orange juice. He nodded and then came beside me and said, "Mom says I need to eat yogurt every morning."

"Got it," I said and grabbed the tub of Greek yogurt. He pointed to a bowl and I let him serve himself.

He was clearly a good kid. He put the lid on and grabbed his own silverware. After he finished, he said, "I need help catching the ball."

"My son?" I said, with my hand pressed to my heart. "After school, why don't you and I throw around a ball?"

"I'd like that." He grabbed his phone on the

table and tossed it at me. "Can you put your number in my phone so I can talk to you?"

I quickly typed my mailing address and phone number. I then asked, "Can I put my parents in there, too? They'd want to meet their grandson."

His eyes widened like I'd just offered him some sacred relic in an adventure film, but he added syrup to his waffle and asked, "Where do they live?"

I passed the butter that he skipped. "Fort Myers, Florida. I see them a lot during spring training."

He didn't take the butter. Georgie must be all about health.

Jeremy asked, "Is that where you're from? The cards say Chicago."

"They moved there when they retired," I answered fast. "And, it's nice to have family around during practice."

He still didn't move for the butter but then turned his phone down on the table and said, "Before I talk to them or you, I'll have to ask my mom."

"Of course," I said cheerily, like that was a non-problem. Georgie was mine and so was Jeremy. Now we'd figure out how to be a family. Last night was my token start when I carried the two sleeping people back to her house from the address she'd given me. I'd found the keys in her back pocket and driven them without waking them much, other than agreeing to stay on the couch, because I needed to take care of them. I jumped up from the table, eager to see Georgie again. "I'll go wake her so she can join us."

"Okay." He sipped his orange juice as birds chirped in the backyard.

I then took to the stairs like I'd been here for years, though I'd spent the night on the couch without exploring much. The hotel had seemed far, and I'd known I'd miss my family. I'd brought slumbering people home in the early morning hours to sleep better and for my son to have a normal routine, not in a hotel.

As I opened her room, the light of the day already streamed in. Georgie's brown hair billowed on her cream pillowcases. And her face without stress as she slumbered was still the same girl that had bewitched my soul years ago. For now, I sat on the edge of her bed and juggled her feet as I said, "Good morning."

She tossed for a minute and sat up, rubbing her eyes as she asked, "Where am I?"

"In your bed." I winked. Today we needed to figure out how our lives melded. Last night, we'd ordered wine, and the sun of the day must have drowsed her as she'd passed out during the massage I'd given her as a way of getting her used to my touch again. And despite how I jiggled her in my arms as I carried her to my car, she hadn't woken.

She'd trusted me enough with her body and our son last night to get them home, and I refused to mess that up. Now she ran her hand through her hair and asked, "What happened last night?"

I scooted closer to her and ran my hand through her soft locks. "I brought you and Jeremy home and had your car brought over an hour ago. I was sure the tow truck would wake you half an hour ago."

"I never sleep this soundly." Her face reddened as she came closer to me and then she pulled back and shook her head as she asked, "Did anything happen between us?"

Part of her soul must have some faith in me, and I'd earn more of that. I jumped off the bed. I was here to build trust. Lust had to take a back seat now. I needed to figure out how Jeremy fit in my life almost as much as I needed to keep Georgie, "You were exhausted and I prefer you awake, willing and open to me."

Her face reddened, but she clasped my hand

like she needed to hold me, but she didn't look at me as she asked, "I passed out? That's not like me."

Good. She remembered how she'd asked me to stay and talk in the morning. I patted her hand and said, "It was late. And you were enjoying the massage."

"Now, that I remember." She glanced up and that sparkle in her eye caught my attention. "I told myself to relax because it was you."

I had to live up to that faith she had at this moment. I didn't move, but the butterflies in my stomach grew. She'd been the only woman I'd wanted for a long time. I sighed and said, "It was partly my fault but seeing you...trust me again... you're worth waiting for."

In the Bahamas where we'd been together, the night before she'd left the hotel, I'd stupidly drank too much, and some woman, Marsha, who didn't matter to me, had flown in from Tulsa and acted like we'd been more than we were. In my inebriated state, I'd not had the chance to explain that well. If that was holding her back, then that conversation had to happen before I seduced her.

And that could be today as there was no reason to wait. Marsha was long gone and had never been important to me.

Georgie took her blue paisley blanket off, and I

saw her naked legs. Last night, I'd peeked when I'd helped her to take her jeans off her for her to sleep better, but I'd stopped myself as she said, "We… look, you're a professional baseball player."

How did that come into this? I nodded as she scooted beside me. "I'm good at my job."

"Jeremy told me." She stood and walked past me toward the bathroom. "You and I…"

"Are complicated," I supplied before she shut the door on me. A moment later, I heard her brushing her teeth. I needed to figure out how to steer this conversation when she came out, but then I heard the doorbell. I snuck downstairs, took the delivery, and brought the jug to her kitchen.

Jeremy watched me with those big blue eyes of his as I poured my coffee into the coffee pot Georgie owned and then hid the rest under the sink.

My boy laughed but didn't say anything, but that smirk that reflected into his eyes was so my father. It was uncanny.

I made a silent return to her bedroom. I closed the door and she flung open the door. My heart raced a little like I'd been caught, "Baseball season isn't all year."

I needed a strategy to get her to agree to quench

my thirst for her when we could and relive the pleasure we'd both had in each other's arms.

She rolled her eyes at me as she grabbed some clothes from her closet and said, "It's pretty much a life. I'm not stupid. Your season is months long and then y'all practice for a few months. You probably get like two months off in the winter."

"That's true." My lips pressed together. Life on the road wasn't easy, but it wasn't forever.

At least she understood some of my life. She came out in a winter white sweater and pants outfit I swear my mom would have worn to a PTA meeting. Georgie didn't even blink as she said, "And, you probably spend it in warm places like the Bahamas."

I helped her with the top button of her shirt though I wanted to rip it off her. The transformation to mother was uncanny and sexy in a new way that hadn't ever crossed my mind. "You never came back."

She lowered her head but didn't step out of my arms. I smelled her rosy scent on me as she said, "I was in mourning, pregnant, and then a single mother. Going back to the hotel in the hopes you might be there was very impractical with low odds and, honestly, seemed like a fantasy life I might lead where I had no responsibilities."

If she'd gone just once in the last six years at the time we'd met, we'd have been together faster. I held her close now and sparks raced through me as I said, "I was there, waiting for you on our anniversary."

She stilled in my arms, then blinked as she asked, "Anniversary?"

I traced her spine up and down. She was even prettier now as she'd lost that girliness and was now all grown woman, fleshed out in all the right places. "Of when we met."

Her face blushed red, and she paused her words, until she said, "Jeremy's in school. Gallivanting off to hotels is for single women, with no worries. It's not like I have parents who might babysit."

We'd figure this out. Her life seemed pretty tame and simple, and we needed to make a deal. "What worries do you have?"

She sucked in her breath, like she didn't want to say whatever was in her mind and then finally said, "Like what do I do if either of us gets sick? Doctors are pricy and my insurance isn't good for more than colds and sniffles and, even then, it sucks."

"Still keep spreadsheets and analyze your decisions that way?"

"Yeah."

Jeremy had seemed healthy this morning. Had he skipped the butter for a reason? I sucked in my breath and said, "Relax."

She met my gaze and massaged my back like she was comforting me over her fears as she said, "Look, I have a great life, but one health crisis can destroy us in a second."

This was her fear? At least my boy was fine. This worry was something I could handle. "I have insurance for Jeremy."

She lifted one shoulder like she wanted to flirt as she had the first time we'd met but then said, "Maybe that DNA test you want is good for something then."

DNA tests don't get him on my insurance alone. More important was us.

I don't know what exactly she'd done since that day we'd lost touch, but I touched her and knew she was mine, forever. For now, she twirled out of my arms and said, "We'll get that as soon as we figure out how to set that up. For now, I'll get breakfast started."

I widened my stance but didn't follow her sexy curves as I said, "Jeremy's eaten. I wanted to ask your permission to bring him to school."

"What?" Instantly she came back to me, but her gaze was unreadable.

They were both important to me. I nodded and repeated as I said, "I want to bring my son to school and see the place."

"My sister works there." Her foot tapped the ground like she needed to put the request in order.

"I'd love to meet her and your entire family."

She nodded and said, "Okay. Olivia is my youngest sister, so starting with her might be okay. We can go together."

Perfect. School started in the morning and training wasn't till late this afternoon. We had time to talk, and we needed to do that. We went down the stairs together. "Give me a minute to eat and we'll head out, in my car."

"Pour me a coffee?" I asked.

"Sure." She took out two glasses.

Jeremy's laugh was on his face, but he turned toward the window as he finished his plate.

I took a seat beside him and tossed a waffle on my plate and one for Georgie. I buttered mine up and waited for her. As she sat at the table with us, my phone rang. I saw my agent's number and stood. Georgie had been an analyst, so she understood numbers mattered, and we'd talk about my own transition soon.

For privacy, I went onto the screened porch and

noticed that some of her neighbors jogged the street. They slowed and stared at me, so I waved but didn't go inside as Phil asked, "What's going on?"

The neighbors moved and I took a seat on her swing. "Good. Some things might be changing for me."

"Okay." He needed to understand about Jeremy and Georgie now, but he continued, "The season is winding down and we're looking at a few offers to weigh. We need to sit down when you get back to Tulsa as money is just one of the benefits to discuss."

"Yeah, we do have to talk."

Georgie had a fear of health care and her analysis of her son's future was what she'd voiced. I could handle Jeremy's insurance now, and if she married me, she'd also be on my plan. The thought hit me as the best deal I could broker. We satisfy our lust and ensure my reputation stays clean for the contract negotiations. I let the thought grow in my head and said, "Include health care in the list of items discussed."

"Are you worried about something?" Phil asked.

I laughed. I was at the top of my game and had enough money in the bank to never worry again if something did, but I shook my head and glanced behind me.

Health was all she'd said she'd feared. It was a starting point for negotiations. Georgie and Jeremy seemed like a dream package as I said, "About my health, no."

"Don't scare me like this, Michael."

Right. I picked at my hair and twirled the small piece as I whispered the truth, "I… I have a son I just found out about. I want to ensure he has health insurance."

"Children's health. Got it. That's usually standard with union contracts anyhow." He said it like it was a relief. "And, a good family life might be good for your image. People still whisper about the hooker who released a book. You are talking about the boy in the Pirates gear and the woman you kissed yesterday?"

I turned and watched as Georgie sipped her coffee and her cheeks brightened as I said, "Yes. I want to marry her, if she'll have me."

"I'll assure the owners the game interruption was a bleep, and you're asking her to marry you. It will assuage some of the press asking questions."

"Georgie is a keeper."

"And you're sure the boy is your son?"

"Yes." I then said, "One question."

"What's that?"

"How's the Pittsburgh offer?"

While my team showed no loyalty to me, the people at the table hopefully would. I needed us all on the same page. Those brown eyes had never left my mind, but then my stomach twisted when he said, "Not one I'm looking at seriously, as it's lower than the others."

There went that thought. I was all about the money now. I nodded and realized sentiment didn't get the best contracts when I said, "Okay. Good to know."

I was about to say goodbye when Phil asked me, "Do you want me to see if they'll up the offer as you'd like to be a Pirate?"

If I was closer to my son, then maybe life would be easier than asking Georgie to pick up and move with me.

She'd probably say no, and she'd be right. I couldn't offer forever when I was on the road a lot. But I asked quietly, "Do you think they'd budge?"

"If you showed interest, maybe. Your son wearing their uniform might be seen as a good thing to their franchise."

We wouldn't get it if we didn't ask, right? I nodded at myself and stared at the two new people in my life that somehow needed to fit in, beyond just an amazing fuck that I knew she was.

I said with heat in my face, "Get me a reasonable number from them and maybe we'll discuss it."

"Good because I thought we were both about the money."

"Oh, we are." I was loyal to my friends on the team, but the team wasn't loyal to me. Money mattered now. I said my "Goodbyes".

Phil's calls were good for the bus or plane rides, but he wasn't what kept me up at night from memories.

That was all the woman in the next room, with my son that I needed to help today.

I came back and scarfed down my waffle. Once I finished, I asked the others, "You ready to head to school?"

Georgie fixed herself a second cup, or maybe third, as I wasn't counting when I'd been on the phone. "This coffee is perfect." She gulped it down and said, "You made it and it's better than mine by far. I've no idea how you managed this."

Jeremy stared at me like he said without words "tell the truth". I tugged at my collar and stood as I said, "I can't lie to you."

"What?"

I took the take-out box and placed it on the counter as I said, "I tried your machine. Your coffee sucked."

She laughed. "That sounds right. It was a clearance bag."

I lowered my head like this was school and I was telling a teacher how I cheated when I said, "So I ordered a decent brand and filled your pot on the stove."

"Let's get Jeremy to school." She checked the lid on the rest of the coffee.

My boy jumped up to join us and we all headed toward her Rav 4. I'd been a kid myself the last time I'd driven to school with a mom, but now I wondered what happened once the kids were off.

Did I finally get my chance to rip Georgie's clothes off?

Chapter 5

Georgie

The principal walked Michael into every class to see Jeremy's teachers. The young women working with my sister, Olivia, batted their eyes at him.

The entire time we walked around the campus, Michael kept his hand on my back.

At least he hadn't shied away from the selfies.

Once we left, I finally breathed. I'd had no idea how many attractive teachers my son had or my sister, Olivia, worked with.

I'm sure she'd text me later, but I silenced my phone for a few minutes. Alone time meant Michael and I could talk.

I'd been living in a bubble yesterday and today.

I wanted him, but I wasn't sure how we fit. Life near him had me on edge and I'd never made smart choices when nervous. Logically, Michael would probably leave forever, so this short time was all I'd get, then I'd be able to breathe.

Except he wanted Jeremy and, after the alluding to more in our conversation, we needed a firm decision if he intended to be in our lives now. And, I needed to get a grip, fast.

Michael and Jeremy might be good together and they deserved that shot. I'd loved my dad, and his cancer was one of the worst times in my life.

Michael held the driver's door for me like a gentleman. Once he joined me in my car, he said, "Jeremy's a good kid."

I nodded but peeled out of the parking lot before someone else stopped us.

I'd like a few hours to talk to Michael and touring a school wasn't my idea of one-on-one time when we had decisions to make about what we wanted to do for our future.

"The school is nice," he said.

I wasn't sure where else to go, so I went on auto-pilot home, until I entered my garage and his two-seater reminded me we didn't fit. I ignored the feeling as I said, "I think so. And he does well in school."

"There are other school options."

"I guess, but I went there myself, so I'm slightly biased into thinking it's a good place."

As the garage door closed, he asked, "Do you think you could live outside of Pittsburgh?"

Tension ran up my back. He wanted us, it seemed, and we'd talk seriously. I turned off the engine and took out my house key while I said, "I never thought about it."

"Why not?" he asked as I turned the key to let him inside.

He went right to the kitchen and poured us more coffee. He'd bought a six-cup container, so we had plenty, and his ass in front of me gave me a nice view. The jeans he wore weren't nearly as tight as his work pants, but I had my memories of his naked body that heated me up. While I'd never believed in love, I'd avoided any mention of sex these past few years. "Why would I?" I asked as I set my purse down. "My family is here."

He placed a cup near my seat from earlier and I took it as he took the seat he'd chosen while he said, "My parents live in Fort Myers. They moved to retire and see me during spring training. They are Jeremy's grandparents, and they'll want to meet you both."

My mind raced faster than my body aching for

his touch did. I'd be lying if I said I didn't want him in my life. I had needs too, and I ignored how I jittered a little and said, "They'll probably be angry about everything."

"That's not their style." He shrugged and said, "I'll handle them. Mostly they'll want to know where they fit."

Good. My parents would have been good for Jeremy. My dad had died before I'd known I was pregnant, and I prayed for years that he was happy I had Jeremy. In a blink, I hoped Michael's parents were good. I wrung my hands together and said, "I don't know. My parents died, so he's only had me, and my sisters, and my cousins, who act like uncles."

"And you all live in Pittsburgh?"

"No." I lowered my head. "Stephanie's living in London now, with her husband-to-be, and my cousins are all over the country."

His eyebrow perked up, but he sipped his coffee. I did the same and, once we finished, he asked, "What about the other four sisters? What happens when they marry?"

I took out my phone to get it out of my pocket and said, "That won't happen."

"How can you know that?"

My stomach tightened. At mom's funeral, steam

had been coming out of me, not tears, and I'd been in my last trimester. Then, I was the first-time mom with a newborn crying hysterically after putting him in his crib. Not honoring that war inside me didn't seem possible. I lifted my chin. "I guess I can't, but we made a pact."

His gaze narrowed. "What pact?"

"To never marry and turn into our mother. She was quite a wallflower."

"Your one sister is breaking that."

His words were like shards of ice he'd plunge into my heart, but I ignored the adrenaline inside me. "She thinks love cures all. I don't know about that."

"They might all change their minds."

We'd never lied to each other as our parents had said the only people you can ever truly rely on is each other. "I don't know."

He stepped closer and his nearness warmed my skin. I glanced up and my lips tingled in anticipation. We both wanted this moment and my heart raced as he said, "Georgie, I'm sure they are pretty, as you're the most beautiful woman I've ever met."

Absolutely sweet. My insides twisted and part of me melted. "Yeah, right. You've met movie stars."

He reached out and took my hand. "Not as glamourous as you think. Most are too skinny."

We stood and he immediately held me closer. I laughed as my breasts pressed into his hard muscles. His hand went lower and I didn't complain at all. "Why do I like when you grab my ass like that?"

"You do," he said, and squeezed it again.

This would go right to the bedroom. Maybe we both needed that. I hadn't been with anyone since, but I wiggled away and picked up our empty cups to bring them to the sink. "Hey, now. We're talking."

"Right." He picked up the sponge and turned on the water to wash the dishes. "I'm sure your sisters have prospects. It could be sooner than you think that it's just you and Jeremy left...unless-"

"No." It was sexy to have him helping like that. I had my hands on my hips, then picked up a towel to dry as I said, "I need to believe my sisters are strong."

He handed me the plates he'd cleaned and asked, "I'm sure they are."

I placed them in the dryer as I wiped my brow and said, "Our mom was weak and none of us want to die of a broken heart or loneliness if some-thing happens to any future husband. I don't want to just wither away and die when I have Jeremy. He needs his mother."

We finished with the cups and he turned off the water as he said, "Your parents sound like they were in love."

"They were that." Love destroyed. I needed peace. My friends all complained about how their parents were awful and sought therapy. But me… all I had were memories with a missing mother figure who never fought for me. Vacations, talking about report cards, and more. My dad teaching me to ride my bike played in my mind as I put a cup down and then met Michael's sexy blue eyes.

My face heated as I was pulled out of the memory and asked, "What?"

He leaned against my counter like he lived here with us and said, "My mother and father are married because religion says divorce is bad, but I don't know if they're happy. They get along, but you must have been raised in gentleness."

True. I would say idyllic, except that crashed and burned with mom. Why had Jeremy, me, or my sisters, not been enough of a reason to live? Maybe marriage should be more of a deal like his parents. I tossed the towel and ignored the beat of my heart as I asked, "Why do you think that?"

He pressed his hand on my back again and said, "Because you're the sweetest woman I ever met."

"Doubtful," I said.

My lips tingled for more kisses and my body roared like I'd denied myself ultimate pleasure last night when I'd passed out.

He lowered his head and pressed his forehead to mine as he said, "Look, about Marsha."

That froze me. The woman in the Bahamas before my mom called that my dad was sick. I remembered the red dress and the high heels clicking on the marble floor as she flounced her hair like she'd replace me in Michael's bed as I asked, "Are you still dating her?"

He held my hand to his heart and said, "No. I didn't date her then. I should have told you that better. I was more worried she'd tell you I was a baseball player, which was stupid on my part."

Now that never crossed my mind and I laughed. I couldn't help it as I said, "I wish she'd spilled that one. Then I'd have tracked you down."

His blue eyes stared at me like he needed to assess me when he said, "She was nothing to me before I met you, and I've never seen her again."

Good. "I hoped there was more to the story than you were a player, but honestly, with my dad's heart attack, I couldn't think about her."

"You were…are everything I want."

Well, I'd not stressed about the details of the other woman from six years ago, but it was good that she wasn't anything to worry about. But I swallowed and asked what bothered me now, "Are you dating anyone?"

His hands traced my sides and held me like he needed me when he said, "No, but I'd like for us to pick up where we started."

Started? In bed and naked, in every corner of that room of his and mine. We'd worn clothes as an accessory to eat out before heading back. That vacation was burned in my mind as my lust-filled dream every night for years now, but I let out a sigh and said, "I…I'm different now."

Mom's don't get to live like that. Responsibility filled my days of working, making lunches to pay for school, cooking dinner, cleaning the house, but he said, "Jeremy's at school and you can take off the mom outfit."

I glanced down at my cardigan and pants and then back at him as I asked, "The what?"

He unbuttoned my sweater as he said, "The PTA, loving mom outfit you wore. We're home, alone."

Alone sounded tempting. And, I'd be in his arms. A huge part of my heart wanted exactly that, but I held still as I said, "You promised to practice catching with my son. Our son."

He tugged my sweater to bring me closer to him. "And we will, after school."

My legs were already jelly, and my breaths were getting shorter. "And what happens when your team leaves? I can't just hope and wait for when your team returns here."

His hands traced my sides and goosebumps grew everywhere. My body remembered his touch, but his words were every reason I shouldn't just strip my clothes off in the kitchen and relive the past when he said, "Unless we both make the play-offs that won't happen and, even then, it's no guarantee as we're not the same division."

My son deserved better. I should want better than to be a stop on the road, but I wasn't sure how Michael fit in my life. He'd said he'd be everywhere and we would live here. He wasn't offering more than moment-to-moment when we fit in his schedule. I'd not be peaceful that way. I reached for his hands and tugged for him to release me when I said, "Then, we shouldn't."

He let go but was still so close that my heart beat in tune with his as he said, "You and Jeremy could be in Tulsa for some of the season."

Flights weren't easy and our lives were built

here. I lowered my lashes and hoped I'd sound calmer. "He has school."

He swallowed and his Adam's apple caught my attention as I remembered how he'd ravaged my body once as he said, "It's late September. This craziness in my life ends, at most, mid-November. Then, we have some time."

I traced the collar of my shirt and asked, "Some time for what?"

He leaned closer and our eyes were in each other's faces as he made my huge kitchen into such a small space as he said, "For you to realize marrying me solves our issues."

Marriage? My ears burned. Sure, I'd had late-night fantasies where Michael found me and Jeremy and we were a family. But he practically shoved peace out the window when I was near him. If we did marry, then I was more than a stopover in his life.

But I wasn't ready to live only for a man and never state my opinion.

I wasn't my mother. I froze as I said, "Wait. What?"

He widened his stance, stepped back and crossed his arms. The huge white kitchen of mine somehow grew back to its normal size as he said, "I can ask for more money in my contracts if there's a stable home life."

"How?"

"My lack of family and the rumors have caused corporate heads to believe I'm volatile. Marriage proves I'm more trusted for the team."

"I see."

"You want health insurance. And Jeremy gets my parents in his life. But it will mean you'll probably have to move from here."

Just pick up my life and follow a ballplayer? This was a leap of faith, but he was my son's father and the only man I wanted. I turned toward the sink as I said, "I can't do this."

He placed his hand on my shoulder and pulses rushed through me as he asked, "Why not?"

I flipped around and his arms caught me as I ignored how my heart now raced. "Because I told you. I refused to get old and die from a broken heart and hurt Jeremy."

His gaze narrowed but he didn't touch me. It was good because I was a total disaster and tears threatened to come. "Then don't. I don't want that."

"What?"

His words stilled me.

Then he touched my sides again like he wanted

to reassure me, but my nipples grew hard as he said, "We have good sex and our lives blend. All you have to do is bend, not that I know the end location of where we'll live yet. And I don't want anything to happen to you if something happens to me. Besides, you have to watch Jeremy."

My mother hadn't cared that she had six girls or twenty of my cousins who'd once considered her their second mother. My son was my everything, but I couldn't deny Michael was the only man I'd ever met who made my body turn into a temple of unending desire. At the moment, his blue eyes were clear and it was all just me being crazy as I straightened out my white pants to loosen any wrinkles and asked, "And, all you want is for me to move with you?"

"I'm a free agent." He took my hand and held it between us as he said, "I don't know where I'll be in the spring. If you marry me, then you're part of the conversation with my agent."

"But you don't want love?" I asked and sucked in my lips. It was a bad habit of mine, like I needed approval when I didn't, but I couldn't stop myself right now. This was another reason a rational deal to satisfy my wants made more sense than some unrealistic belief that love fixes everything.

He blew out that sexy mouth of his and he said

clear as daylight, "Fuck, no. I just want you, in my bed again, and to get more money. Stable players who don't court trouble get higher offers. And, I want you to outlive me."

A few fish kisses on blind dates that only confirmed I hadn't needed them.

I needed Michael's touch. No one else had ever come close to making me feel…this sexy. I reached out and ran my fingers over his stubble and said, "Let's see how this winter works, and then we'll talk about it more."

A grin showed on his face as he started to take my sweater off. "That's a start. Now let's get this outfit off you. We won't wrinkle it."

My fingers traced against the fuzz on his face. My skin radiated as I let his face go and curled my arms around his short hair. "We won't?"

"No." He tugged it off me and then placed it on a chair behind him as he said, "You'll want to look like a good mom in this outfit when we pick our boy up."

This morning was crazy. I held my hands up as he lifted my shirt off my body and laid it with my sweater. "If you make it out of school. I'm sure Jeremy told everyone about your practice, and you didn't get to meet Olivia."

He then returned to my side and unzipped my

pants as he said, "Good. I want my boy to be happy, after I make his mom and me happy, too."

If he was anything like I remembered, then I'd not know my own name in a few minutes. But I needed to relive the past right now as seven years was too long and his lips on mine burned through to my soul, reminding me I was already his.

I always had been.

Chapter 6

Michael

Georgie was somehow even better. Maybe because I'd waited all this time.

Finally, my cock found the perfect glove that fit and had never wanted to trade for another. She had no idea the power she possessed over me. I hadn't believed sex could create monogamy in me, not until I'd lived the past few years.

Maybe I was in love already and had been since we met.

The explosion of sheer joy with my Georgie couldn't be replicated.

I collapsed beside her, but I felt someone

shaking me and I opened my eyes and stared into her brown ember hues.

Tension rushed up my spine and adrenaline poured through me with these thoughts. She had zero idea with that pout as she said, "Get dressed."

I rubbed my eyes and said, "Is it time to get you all proper…" But I looked at her and my stomach twisted. She was Ms. PTA again. I stretched and slumped my shoulders. "Aww, I missed my chance for a second go."

"Later." She tossed my jeans at me and said, "You promised Jeremy you'd teach him to catch."

Right. And I needed to be a stable family man to earn that paycheck I wanted. My agent said stability earned more contract money.

I wiggled into my jeans and stood to finish. She flounced to the door and I called out, "Let me grab my shirt."

My shirt was halfway across her floral bedroom. Once we married, if she agreed, we'd have to ditch the blue paisley. I'd compromise on most patterns, but not so bright and bold, or lace curtains…simple was always better.

I ran out of the room, down the stairs, and grabbed my sneakers near the door as she headed to the car. As I jumped in to join her, she clicked the unlock button and asked me, "Any chance you could make Pittsburgh your home base?"

"They lowballed their offer," I answered.

What I'd told her about love was fucking right, though. We needed to keep this stable family and stay good in bed. Love was messy and complicated for her. Monogamy and sex were a start, and she already had that with me. We'd have years to figure out feelings, or she could deny them forever, as long as she stood beside me.

She turned on her car, clicked a button to open her garage, and we peeled out like we were already a family as she asked, "So where's most likely?"

Hopefully, this meant she was thinking about what I offered as I said, "I told Phil I didn't care, and he could just tell me the team names once we've gone over the numbers and perks with the offers."

She tapped the steering wheel like she was listening to a song only she could hear. "What kind of numbers are we talking about?"

There was my spreadsheet analyst. I turned to watch her face as I discussed numbers while she drove. "I want 30 million a year with a guarantee of five to ten years, then I retire."

She sucked in her lip and her face reddened a little. Then she continued to tap the wheel like she was unfazed and said, "So you're talking 150 million to 300 million?"

Good. She'd understand that kind of money was worth being a little up in the air about a home. This was why I needed to be mobile, and it wasn't forever. I nodded and said, "If it's five years, I'd have to negotiate again, possibly, but I'm not going more than ten. I want a ten-year guarantee."

"It's double." She said without even glancing at me.

We pulled up into some line and we started inching forward slower than a snail in a race. But she didn't turn off the car, which meant she expected to move.

"It means I could retire when Jeremy is sixteen and then stay home with you and fuck you all day, every day until we tire, like that week in the Bahamas."

Her cheeks blushed prettily, and she glanced at me, then moved the car a little, as she said, "Well, that is a picture that will live in my mind." We stopped in front of a walkway and she stiffened and said, "But here we need to be good."

She unlocked her door to get out and said, "That's my sister with Jeremy."

"Olivia?"

"That's her name."

Jeremy held hands with a smaller, skinnier version of my Georgie. I followed her out of the car as the young woman hugged her sister and said, "Georgiana."

Georgie stepped back and patted my arm, standing next to me like we were now in some competition together as she said, "Olivia, this is Michael Irons. He's Jeremy's father."

Olivia stilled but then offered her hand to shake and said, "The mystery is finally solved. Nice to meet you."

I shook it but asked as I glanced at Georgie, "What mystery?"

Olivia said, "We've all wondered who in the world my sister had been with and never talked about. We all guessed you were special to her as she never said a word about you, but when she'd gone to college, she'd ranted all about her then-boyfriend, Osmand, who'd broken her heart."

"Ozzie? I'd forgotten about him entirely. I think he went to law school."

She didn't sound torn up, so I let that go. I'd had girlfriends before I'd met Georgie and, honestly, she had a right to move on with her life these seven years, though I was glad she was free now.

Georgie turned white, like she'd faced an execution, as I said, "It's nice to meet one of Georgie's five little sisters."

Her sister placed her hand on her hip and tossed her hair back as she said, "So you knew about us. Will we be seeing you around?"

Georgie opened the backdoor for Jeremy to get in as I said, "If Georgie here agrees to marry me like I asked."

Both sisters shared an exchange I didn't get, but it was clear an unspoken conversation had just happened. Then Georgie buckled our boy in with the click as he asked, "Mom, you're marrying Michael?"

I waved and opened my door as Georgie then came over, hugged her sister and said, "We got to go. See you later, Olivia."

I closed my door and leaned over to open hers. She got in and closed the driver's door without a word. A few minutes later, we were back on the road, away from the school and Jeremy asked, "Mom?"

My heart stilled as I stared at her profile. Her jawline was clear as she watched the road and simply said, "It's not been decided."

She hadn't even looked at me.

Jeremy didn't seem fazed by her avoidance and asked, "Why not?"

She turned and softened her gaze as she winked at our boy and then glanced at me as she said, "It's complicated."

Jeremy threw his hands up in the air, making my arguments for me as he asked, "How is everything complicated with you?"

Later I'd have to talk to him. Women were a mystery no man has ever fully understood. My own father had explained that to me and, only now, I understood I'd get to pass that tidbit on as she said, "Because…I have to think about it."

I winked at her, not that she saw me when I said, "Think fast."

I asked my boy as we neared his home, "Are you ready to practice?"

As we pulled onto her small street, Jeremy's face reddened and he said, "My friends wanted to know if they could come and learn, too."

Georgie opened her home without a word and asked, "How many?"

"The whole team?" He asked as his voice squeaked.

We parked and she opened the door. I found my phone and turned it on as I said, "Let me make a phone call."

"Okay." He said and we all filed inside.

Phil had called as had a few of the team. I

quickly called our manager and stayed in the background of her kitchen as Georgie handed our son a snack and said, "So I have some little leaguers in need of practice."

Jeremy watched me and my shirt neck felt tighter until the manager said what I hoped. Good. I relaxed and met his gaze while I said, "Perfect."

I had to wait a second to listen to the schedule and once I hung up, Jeremy asked, "So?"

I placed my phone on the table and nodded like I could offer him the world as I said, "The Sooners will happily help your team if they show up in an hour to the stadium..." My phone beeped and I picked it up to read as I said, "Hold on." I patted Jeremy's side and told him fast, "Text your friends. Free parking for moms." I quickly typed my team manager and then turned off the phone. Family time was now and it wouldn't be interrupted anymore. But I said, "Okay, Pirates are helping too and whoever shows up gets free tickets to tonight's game."

Georgie brought over cut apple slices and placed them in front of my son as she said, "That's pretty awesome. Text Aunt Olivia, too, sweetheart."

Jeremy did as asked and I grabbed one of the crunchy healthy snacks she'd made. Once finished, he met my gaze and asked, "Michael?"

"Yeah, Buddy," I said fast. The idea this boy was mine somehow made my shoulders bigger, like I had reason to be proud.

He put his phone down and said, "I don't want to look bad out there."

Right. I was here to help and pointed toward his backyard and said, "You'll need a haircut as your hair is getting in the way of seeing, but you and I will practice one-on-one until the others get there."

Georgie clutched her heart like she was happy as we went out.

Jeremy wasn't bad. He played like he loved the game. Once, I'd been like him, and my dad pushed that love into a passion to be the best. I talked like my own dad once did with me about watching the other players moves to anticipate action, and how everyone would judge him differently now that it was known he was my son. He got it and jumped with more enthusiasm when I tossed the ball.

A haircut would be fast, but I didn't want to bug Georgie for clippers. Tomorrow before we shipped out, that was on the agenda, even if he missed some school.

The alarm rang and I knew we had to go. We came back in and Georgie was now wearing shorts that went to her knees, a pink cardigan, and a clingy t-shirt underneath. Fields get hot, but I didn't argue. We filed into her Rav 4 and headed to the stadium.

Jeremy now wore a plain gray shirt to go along with his jeans.

I tried to give Georgie space in my seat, though we were still close in proximity.

Plus, my body was still relieved after six years of waiting. I directed them where to park and pointed toward the parking signs for the kids. As we unbuckled in our spot, I walked with my family down the player row where press waited for us so I could direct them to family seating. As we stood near reporters, I hugged both closer and said, "Okay. We're here. Walk fast."

A woman from a sports network threw her microphone in Georgie's face as she asked, "So how did you and Irons meet?"

She kept up pace with me. "Years ago."

The reporter then said, "That doesn't answer the question."

Georgie took my hand and held it as lights flashed at us and she said, "I-"

I interrupted and directed them toward the door as I took the direct line of questions when I said, "Georgie and I were in love, but then her father and mother died. We've had a difficult road, but I'm hoping that's over and she marries me now."

Georgie squeezed my hand, glanced at my profile, and said, "I...I'm going to say yes."

"You are?" My skin electrified and my hairs stood on the ends. I stilled and rationalized instantly that this was about the money we'd discussed. It had to be, as she didn't believe in love.

Money was the root of everything, so I shouldn't be surprised, even if coldness hit the back of my neck at the thought. I probably shouldn't be excited about the future if this was just about money and security.

Georgie said as I opened the door for the players, "Yeah. I think we should take the next step and make it official."

I almost closed the door on the reporters, but the woman from earlier asked, "So, no more prostitutes, Michael?"

"Absolutely not," I said. No one had ever believed I hadn't touched that woman. I didn't care, except I didn't want that discussion near Jeremy or to rehash it with Georgie. I waved as the door closed, "We have to get going."

Jeremy asked me as we strolled through the locker room, "What were they talking about, Michael?"

I grabbed a Sooner's hat for my son and pushed his hair behind his ear as I said. "Nothing that matters. Sometimes people make up stories to help themselves feel better, and it's important to not always listen to the news about me. You and your mom need to trust me."

"Okay," he said while I gloved him up with a professional version he could keep. "In school, Bobby once said I ate black beans because I loved farting. Everyone laughed at me."

I patted his shoulder and said, "Exactly the same."

He nodded at me. As I tightened the license, I met his mother's gaze and said, "I'll get you a ring, Georgie."

"I don't need one," she said fast.

For better or worse, they were mine. And, no one was going to interfere with that, but as I stood, I patted her backside and said, "After the game, we need to talk."

She nodded like she agreed but then went with her son to meet the other kids. I motioned to my manager and he gave me a thumbs-up.

This was for publicity and to show I was a dedi-cated family man. Using my son's team to earn myself $30 million a year was fine. It had to be.

Georgie and I were taking the money and that

didn't include real love, just the kind we talk about on TV when others are watching, at least for her. One day, I might tell her she was always the one for me, when she might believe that love doesn't destroy her voice and we'd be fine.

Today was not that day.

Chapter 7

Georgie

The game went on and on.

He wore his sexy gray pants that showed off his ass on the field, which kept me from paying any attention to the game at all.

I kept my head high, but during the fifth inning, Michael rushed over to me and my heart pitter-pattered like I was a little kid about to get a present.

He grabbed my arm and said, "I've been thinking about our son's game while I've been playing."

"Seriously?"

"We need to get Jeremy a haircut."

Okay, so that wasn't exactly romantic, but I tilted my head and asked, "Why?"

He ran his hand through Jeremy's hair and said, "He can't see from the locks you have on the side. That is why he is having problems catching the ball."

I glanced down at my son's dirty blonde hair. "His cute, angelic locks that he wanted."

Jeremy picked at his locks the way Michael played with his own tiny piece of hair and said, "Up to him, but if he wants to catch and throw correctly, we'll need to shave that off. He needs to see."

"I want to if it helps."

"Okay," My heart thudded. On the field, he thought about us and Jeremy's needs. Part of me was flattered.

My son's eyes had tears that washed down his upturned cheeks and a glow I'd not seen in him before.

Guess they'd talked about it. My mind had been in a cloud for hours now. After saying I'd marry Michael, I'd been dazed, but I was just now focusing.

Michael jogged back to his dugout, and I returned my attention to my son, his team, their parents, and tried to sip my soda.

A minute later, Deena fluffed her curly black hair behind her head. My nose almost winced from the perfume she exuded. I ignored the fact that her hair didn't quite blow despite the wind. She gave me a once over, held a hot dog, then said like we were friends, "Georgiana, this is lovely what you've done for the boys."

I put my drink down into the holder and stood as Michael was retaking the field. He was short-stop, so he wasn't near me, but it was weird for the kids around me that seemed torn to not be rooting for the home team, but none of them said anything to me as I just said, "I didn't do anything special. Michael invited us all."

Jeremy screamed like he'd woken up Christmas morning when Michael caught the ball.

Michael fist pumped the pitcher near him.

Deena bit into her hot dog and finished chewing while staying near me, like she was one of my sisters. As she finished, she said, "So you've been dating a baseball player for years. No wonder we couldn't set you up with Andrew."

Right. Andrew, the widower with five small children and a bald head, who hadn't been looking for a wife so much as a babysitter to relieve him of duty. Deena's set up had been an horrendous mistake, and I avoided discussing dating with her, but now I said only, "Michael's...well, Michael's pretty special to me."

Deena finished her hot dog then said, "If you're looking to be more involved at school, you have our vote."

My heart raced a little more as I asked, "Vote?"

"For PTA president," she said.

Wait. My son loved his team and the game. Today's invitation wasn't political, but I shook my head. My soda dripped on the ground as I wasn't drinking it and the ice melted more while I tried to find the words. Then I glanced over at Michael, who expected me to move, and said, "Oh, I can't. My sister's a teacher there."

Deena pinched my side and said, "You doing things like this for our boys... you're the clear leader here."

"This is just for the team, not the school." That wasn't what this was. I was here for Jeremy...and Michael. I crossed my legs and remembered how complete I was when he rammed inside me, not that I would ever, ever, ever say that out loud. I shrugged and said, "I don't know. It's a big time commitment."

Deena's nose went up in the air as she said, "You can do it. You're working part-time, minimum wage at that store, and now we know how you afford that."

Deena's assumptions about my life were wrong. My skin prickled as I just stared at her and asked, "Excuse me?"

She leaned closer and pretended we were just best buddies as she said, "You've been in that big house, alone, and we've all wondered."

The practice inning ended and Michael's water boy motioned toward me. I politely told Deena, "I have to go," and went to speak to Aaron, who delivered a message. I was to take Jeremy and go with Aaron after the top of the ninth of the real game.

I nodded and returned to my seat. Thankfully, she was gone.

Good. Jeremy returned and hugged me like today was his birthday. My son hugged less frequently these days, so I took my moment.

Done, we settled into our seats for the game and the sun went down, but soon the appointed hour came. Once the game ended, Michael walked over to me as the other men filed further in where we couldn't see. I wrapped my arm around his neck that was slightly sweaty now as I said, "Congrats."

He hugged me but stared at my face when he asked, "What's wrong?"

Deena. I let out a long breath and said, "I was just insulted but ignored it."

He picked up my chin and stared at me when he said, "Good. Pennsylvania has a waiting period, so I want us to fly to Vegas tomorrow. There is a 6:30 AM nonstop that gets us there by 9:00. We can be married before 3:00 and we can catch a flight to Tulsa for the 7:00 game."

During the game, he'd searched for tickets? I held my breath, but his blue eyes were like sirens that dared me to do something out of character. Michael's offer made my pulse skip. I nodded and said, "You researched this."

He wrapped his arms around me and kissed me.

I heard applause somewhere, but I thought maybe I imagined it. As the kiss ended, the sound roared in my ear, but he let me go and said, "Think about it. Jeremy misses a day of school, but you and he can be back by Monday morning. I have to go shower and interview. Meet me near the parking lot."

"We'll be there," I said and turned around to see all the parents and other children in Jeremy's school staring at us.

The kids looked horrified, but the mom's seemed…jealous. I fiddled with my hair and held my son's hand. That was a bad thought. I waved at them and we followed Aaron out of the stands.

This time, I didn't want to wait in the dressing room, so we headed to my car. He knew to join us, so I wasn't worried about whatever he said to reporters, though as Jeremy jumped into his seat, he asked, "Mom, were you serious about marrying Michael?"

"I think I am," I said, and double-checked the passenger seat was clean for Michael.

I started to close his door when he said, "Maybe I'll feel comfortable calling him dad, then."

I slumped my shoulders and took my seat. When I closed my door, I turned back toward him and said, "You don't need my wedding to do that."

"I guess." He shrugged. "I love hanging out with Michael, a lot."

"I'm sure he likes you, too."

I buckled my own seat and turned the engine on. I didn't need Jeremy feeling like he needed to defend me from Michael. Marrying him would hopefully help Jeremy feel secure. But I wasn't sure what to say either, so I played music.

A few minutes later, Michael slipped into the seat beside me, wearing jeans, a black t-shirt that clung to those ab muscles of his, and his hair still wet. "You both ready?"

I glanced in my mirror. Jeremy was paying attention to his father like he'd worship him. I asked, "Do you want to go to your hotel or home?"

I reversed out of my spot to get us out as he said, "Home, with you, unless you don't want me to?"

"No, home is good," I said and focused on my driving. Maybe getting married was a good idea. Jeremy gained a father, health insurance, and I had amazing sex with Michael. All of that added up to a pretty good life.

Michael took out his phone. "I'll have my things sent over, so I have them to hit the road when I return the rental to the airport."

This was finite unless we went to Vegas. The idea of hopping on a plane with him had adrenaline pulsing inside my skin. Or maybe it was that he was here again with me. Jeremy broke the silence. "So what do you usually do after a game?"

He glanced back, "I normally hit the hotel gym."

After spending hours in the hot sun, the last thing I wanted to do was work out. And he'd played hard out there. I navigated the backroads to my home, "Why?"

He glanced at my breasts and my body warmed. "I have a lot of pent-up energy inside my body still. I found working out calmed me down to sleep."

My body heated from his perusal as my son said, "We don't have a gym at home."

Michael smiled brighter and glanced at our son. "It's fine. Having Georgie and you safe and home is perfect. I'll find another way to get rid of my over-drive of energy from adrenaline." He winked at me and my face warmed.

No one said anything as I parked next to the two-seater rental car and opened the kitchen door. As we locked the door behind us and took off our sneakers, Jeremy waved us off. "I'm going to shower and go to bed."

I called behind him as I placed shoes in the rack properly, "Jeremy, pack a bag for a few days."

He stopped midstride and stared at me as he asked, "Why?"

I stood and widened my stance. "We're going to Tulsa and Vegas."

"No school?" Jeremy's lips curled high on his cheeks.

Michael nodded at me, but his face was more mysterious as I told Jeremy, "You miss a day. I'll write you a note."

Michael went down on one knee. "I'd like permission to marry your mom from you."

My heart thundered a little differently as I pressed my hand to my heart.

"My... yeah, I'd like that." Jeremy hugged Michael and my heart melted a little.

Michael stood and Jeremy shrugged like this wasn't a big moment and headed up the stairs as he waved behind him. "Night, Mom. Night, Michael."

Right. Hopefully, my son grew more confident near Michael the more they spent time together. Hopefully, in time, combining our family would help Jeremy trust both his parents, which was important, and was another reason to agree to our wedding. He needed a strong male figure in his life. My dad had been the heart of my own family growing up. As the door closed upstairs, I opened the refrigerator and took out a bottle of wine for us as he said, "He's struggling with calling you 'dad'."

"It's only been two days." Michael went to my cabinets and grabbed two glasses for us as he said, "He can take his time. I'm not pushy, though my parents want to meet him."

So he'd talked about me to his parents, too? I didn't ask, but I finished pouring and ignored how my skin was slightly jumpy and sipped my wine. Michael did the same and, as I finished, I asked him, "Will that be this weekend, as well?"

He gave me a smirk and put his glass down on the counter as he hugged my waist and said, "No. They live in Florida, not Oklahoma. I need to tell you my house isn't kid-friendly."

"It's okay. We'll manage." Jeremy wasn't a toddler anymore.

I soon lost sight of where I was, except in Michael's arms. I asked Michael, "Now, tell me, what happened at the game that had you thinking 'Vegas'?"

I put that in air quotes to emphasize.

"It's nothing. Though, someone set you off at the game?" He asked, and his gaze melted my tension.

I ignored how goosebumps grew on my arm and glanced down at how our bodies touched as I said, "One of the parents thought I'd been living off your money the whole time."

His hand traced my back as he said, "That's stupid."

Well, it wasn't that. I sucked in my bottom lip and then let it out as I knew that was a horrible habit of mine and said, "I don't tell people about my inheritance. It's no one's business."

He cupped my face as I was lost in his gaze. His words melted me like chocolate in a pan, "No one needs to know how you drive me wild, either."

"I do?"

"Hell, yes."

I tugged on his waist and tugged him toward me when I said, "Wait until we're in our bedroom."

Then, I let him go. He took the glasses and wine and followed me as I led up the stairs.

Having Michael Irons at my call sent a thrill through me. I knew he watched and I took the next few steps with more a sway to my hips and opened the door.

He closed the door and placed the still filled wine glasses and the bottle on my bureau.

And then his arms wrapped around me.

I was alive with him, in a way I never was, ever. I ached. He unzipped his pants and let them fall as I slipped my plain shirt off me.

My heart raced as I unsnapped my own jeans and tore them off as he tossed his shirt next to his pants.

Then he peeled off my bra, so I was just in my panties when his lips claimed my mouth for a kiss that burned into my soul

Nothing about being with Michael was calming.

Michael made me forget my inhibitions and a thrill raced through me like I loved to follow through on dares. And his lips went lower, my body trembled as he sucked my nipples into his mouth.

I arched to give him more and, as he released my chest, he laughed and said, "Your breasts are just the beginning."

He walked me backward toward the bed. His cock was roaring to life like the bat he'd held in his arms earlier tonight.

His face was just as hard as he motioned with his head and said, "I've been fantasizing of taking you near that bedroom window of yours that over-looks the street."

"Hmm, guess you'd better seduce me into that," I said and climbed on the bed.

Maybe later, we'd get daring. Tonight, I just wanted him, inside me, so I tossed my panties, he tossed his tighty-whities, and joined me on the bed.

Marrying Michael hopefully meant we'd have more of this release and I'd figure out how to remain calm and peaceful the rest of the time. When he touched me, I was already in a crescendo of desire that rocked through my entire body and I lost the ability to think.

Chapter 8

Michael

We got up way too early, but with Jeremy sleeping, and everyone only having a small bag, I tucked everything in the back and carried my sleeping son. One day soon, this wouldn't just be for the sex and the money for her, but I'd have to convince her to open her heart.

Georgie was half-asleep herself, but she got in the car, helped with the airport where she showed Jeremy's birth certificate. The spot for the father's name was blank.

I cringed and hoped we could get that paper-work fixed.

I hadn't asked to fix it or anything that required thinking this early. The moon was still in the sky when we shuffled through getting to the plane.

As we approached the terminal gate, I'd guessed I'd been recognized, but I kept my head down.

A boy three years older than Jeremy approached for an autograph and selfie. If I got the contract I'd wanted, soon we'd book a private plane, if we wanted. For the next few minutes, I was standing with the agents to sign boarding passes as autographs and take selfies.

Normally, I flew first class, but Southwest had no option. So, this morning I pasted on my smile.

Three hours into the flight, Georgie'd had enough sleep and coffee that she sat up. I'd scouted wedding packages while she'd been out of it and now she said, "We're lucky he slept."

They were both here with me, so everything was good, no matter what. If we ended up at a drive-through wedding and not one of the packages, I'd not complain too much. I'd have my family, but I put my coffee on her tray for her and said, "I'd have flown you first-class, but the first nonstop plane was first come, first served."

"Next time." She lifted her cheeks in that pretty smile of hers that made everything near her shine brighter. "We didn't mind holding our seats as you autographed boarding passes."

I showed her on my phone the packages I'd found as I said, "We're almost at Vegas. Do you have a wedding theme you want?"

She scrolled the pages and said, "I am digging the gondola ride." She pointed toward our son. "Would Jeremy be able to join us?"

His face was plastered to the plastic wall.

I nodded. "He's on the small side. He can share my seat."

The plane started the descent.

"It sounds pretty," Georgie said.

Chosen then. The captain hadn't said anything, so we had a few minutes. I typed in my credit card information and picked the package options, as she sipped the coffee. I finished right when the captain said, 'No Electronics' or whatever the spiel about descent is, but I held my phone a moment longer until I saw the confirmation page. "Done. It's booked."

She locked arms with me. As we landed, I said, "We get a two-night stay, but we can't take that right now. When baseball season ends, in November, if we make the playoffs, we can decide where we want a proper honeymoon."

"That's a lot of detail." She ran her hands

through her brown hair. The plane was finally nearing land. "So what was included in that package you booked on the flight?"

I checked on my son who pivoted his head from the wall to his mother's side as I said, "We have the wedding, the lunch, the limo to and from the hotel, so we just need a ring and a dress, and you have two hours at the spa to get yourself ready. Less, if taking the dress takes more than an hour. Once we finish, we have to get right back to the limo for the flight to Tulsa, so I can be there for the home game."

"Got it. You are a planner," she said as the wheels hit the ground.

Once we pulled into a gate, I said, "With details taken care of, we get better service and what we expect, without guessing."

"I normally consult spreadsheets to make decisions, but at least you plan something. I'd panic if the plan was to show up and just see what's available."

I remembered that detail about her already, but her comfort with me was good.

We'd have a good life together and taking care of my family made me feel more grounded.

A few minutes later, we were off the plane. I

held Georgie's hand and she led our son with her other. Her hands were soft but capable as she said, "Jeremy will be bored if I'm getting hair, makeup, and a dress."

"He can come with me." The limo drove to pick us up, so we headed right to the Venetian, where they had everything for us in one place.

"What will you both do while I'm off getting pampered?"

One of the perks I'd offered, but the word pampered rubbed my skin like sandpaper. I said as I realized Jeremy was listening to music, "We'll get our tux's and he can help me pick out a ring and check everything is in order."

We stepped inside, but she lowered her voice as the driver took off, so only I heard her, "You and he haven't spent any time alone."

"Until now." I pressed my forehead to hers. I wanted my son to trust me just as I needed Georgie to. "We're about to be a family."

"Sounds good," she said.

I nodded and said, "Perfect."

The limo went to the front and she tugged the earbuds out as she said, "Jeremy, take those off."

"What's going on?" He asked and put his head-phones away.

The driver opened my side and I slipped out as I said, "We're at the hotel now."

I waited near the door and took her hand. Jeremy saw us and his face was red. "Did I miss the wedding?"

We headed inside the hotel and went toward the wedding reception desk as I said, "No, you and I need to go find a ring and get tuxes."

I gave my name and the girl behind the desk typed it in the computer. Then, two women came for Georgie in their uniforms and she hugged us both. I kissed her cheek though she hadn't offered her lips as she said, "Have fun, you guys."

Jeremy stood next to me with his hands in his pockets, but his face was white as he asked, "Where is mom going?"

I tilted my head and then mimicked his body stance though my back went tight. I never slouched, but I said, "To get a dress, her hair, and makeup. Do you want to go with her or come with me to do the guy stuff like getting our clothes and picking out the ring for her? You know her better, so I'd need your help and, if you come with me, you can help pick out your own clothes."

"I like picking out my own clothes." I stilled. I'd hoped we'd get a few minutes to ourselves to get to know him, but I held my breath until I heard the words, "Bye, Mom."

Good. My chest poofed out a little that my son wanted to come with me. I'd ensure he had a good time. After she left, the wedding staff directed us toward a store and mentioned they'd taken Georgie to Nieman Marcus for a dress.

I insisted the charges were mine and the staff promised to take care of everything. I walked beside my boy and heard Jeremy as we walked into the suit shop, "Michael, thanks for letting me come. I've never been to a wedding."

Near the tuxedo shop, I spotted an ice cream shop in the mall area, which would be fun to check out, if we had the time. "Glad you're here. You're my son. I'm hoping you and I get closer the more we spend time together."

His face was red, but he nodded. "That sounds good. I'd like that."

A few minutes later, we both came out wearing matching black suits with white tops. Two different tailors worked on us to keep the fitting on schedule, as Jeremy said, "I always wanted mom to marry."

I stilled as I didn't want my son to think weddings were twice or more and said, "She's only marrying me, your father. So this is a one-time thing."

He laughed like I'd just said a funny joke but then quieted down and said, "Good, because her and my aunts and uncles, all saying they don't want to ever marry just made me sad."

"Uncles?"

"I guess they are my mom's cousins, but I call them my uncles. Mom said they are like her brothers because, at one point, they all lived together when they were little."

Cousins and siblings would be nice. I'd never had any. Her parents' deaths were clearly hurtful for her. Hopefully, in time, the wedding would be a dream for both of us and not just about the money for her. I knelt down despite the pins and said, "They said that, and you heard?"

The tailor tugged for me to stand, but I only moved when Jeremy started talking and staring like I'd just started a revolt. "Yeah. They said they'd never be like my grandma and die without living. I don't want my mom to be sad and lonely when I go to college one day."

College had been fun, where I'd finally signed for recruiting into a farm system. I'd finished my degree online during my rookie year, and that was why I'd gone to the Bahamas to celebrate. Then, I'd met Georgie, so it was part of the cycle. I tugged my ear and then the tailor tapped that he was done. I beamed with pride at how handsome Jeremy was when I said, "Thanks for sharing. She mentioned a little, but I hadn't thought it ran that deep."

Tuxedos were done and alterations had taken an hour. Hotel security guided us to a jewelry shop and mentioned Georgie was now in the spa.

I suspected she'd be on time.

The diamonds were big, but Georgie was my princess, so I went with one of them and a simple gold ring that I'd have to match.

I asked my son, "What do you think of this one?"

"It's cool," he said. "Mom said she loved my Aunt Stephanie's ring and that was way smaller."

That was all I'd get. I paid and we headed back when the wedding staff took us back to the store. Time was flying today. We only had ten minutes now. We rushed in the tux shop, where I said, "Then let's get dressed. It's time to meet your mom."

We dressed and the staff helped us with our hair for two minutes. Mine was short, so there wasn't much to comb. I went down to one knee and asked, "Do you want to cut those sides so you can see the ball better when you play?"

"I heard you talking to Mom at the game. You think my hair is why I can't catch well?"

"Yeah."

"Do it." He nodded at me and stood like a soldier.

I took the clippers from the girl and shaved the edges myself and then handed it back for her to finish his cut.

As she finished, Jeremy stared up at me. I patted him on the back and said, "You're even more handsome now."

He beamed at me like I'd just given him the biggest gift out there.

Jeremy walked beside me and, again, I saw my father in his face. We made it to the bridge and saw the lineup for the gondolas. The wedding staff directed us to a side entrance, and toward a waiting boat with a minister.

"Is this a boat?" Jeremy asked as we jumped in.

He put his weight back and forth to shake the boat and then as I reached him, he put his head over the side and checked that there was water or something. He sat in his seat like he was fine a moment later.

I leaned forward. "Your mom said she wanted to get married on the gondola. She wanted privacy."

He took his phone out of his pocket and asked, "Can I take a picture to send to my aunts and uncles?"

"Yeah," I said. The wedding staff was moving. Finally, I'd have the only woman in my heart as mine for a lifetime. This was good. I stood in the boat and saw the silk and lace and then locked gazes with Georgie's brown eyes. "Your mom is breathtaking."

She was a vision as she came toward me and my chest was tight. As she reached the boat, she held her hands out and asked, "Can you two help me step down?"

"Absolutely." I reached past her poofy dress at the bottom and glanced at her now white jeweled figure on display as I held her to get her down.

She fixed my bowtie and then our son's. "You both look great. Nice haircut."

"Michael did it."

"Jeremy agreed and we discussed it."

"We did."

I helped her to her seat as she slightly rocked the boat.

"And you're beautiful, Georgie."

"It's the makeup," she said and glanced away.

"No, it's you. You're beautiful."

Her face had a blush, but she didn't argue.

The officiant then pointed toward me and her as he said, "You two take that seat. Jeremy, sit next to me while I get your parents married."

And, in a dream, a few minutes later, I said yes, and we were married.

We had a shot at forever now, if she'd let us.

Chapter 9

Georgie

"You may now kiss the bride," the officiant said and my eyelids fluttered closed.

I forgot my son was watching when Michael claimed his kiss. Goosebumps grew on my arms, and I ran my fingers through his hair.

This was a sweet moment, and I hardly heard my son's groan or the gondola driver's singing.

I belonged to Michael, forever.

No tears, not now. I needed to be calm and this wasn't it.

Back in the Bahamas, I'd imagined him as my husband, but that dream had disappeared, until now, as his kiss ended.

Now the dream was visceral and staring me in the face. And my gaze got misty.

A memory came of sitting at my mom's funeral, where my sisters, cousins, and I all swore that love and happily-ever-after were lies that we'd never believe again. Everyone agreed, and I'd sworn with my sisters to never love any man so much that I'd want to stop living if something happened to him. My cousins probably had other reasons for agreeing, as it had been my dad that took them in at some point in our lives.

All of us had made a pact. Stephanie broke the bond first when she announced she was getting married.

The tension in my back, like I had betrayed my sisters, made my face heat.

And Michael, maybe he didn't count, because I'd been with him before the vow and our wedding wasn't about love. It was about keeping Jeremy's future secure, forever.

The gondola docked and he held my hand and helped me get off the boat as I wiped my eyes and said, "This was beautiful."

He had his hand on my back and Jeremy's to lead us through a small walkway as he said, "Don't cry. We have lunch."

Tears came out, like marrying Michael was

wonderful, and I said, "Don't comfort me. You don't make me calm at all and I'll cry more."

I don't even know why, and I couldn't analyze it. The staff directed us to follow them to a room. He massaged me and said, "Let's change fast."

We were brought to a hotel room where our clothes were bagged up, and boxes were laid out. Jeremy picked up his and said, "Mom, Michael bought me a new outfit."

Like he'd done for me, too. The dress hadn't been cheap, not that any wedding dress was. But I let Michael unzip me and my spine had a zap of awareness as Jeremy said, "My aunts and uncles all agree you were beautiful."

My son's voice was like cold water tossed in my face as I asked, "You told them?"

Jeremy's eyes widened and said, "I took a video and put it in the group chat."

My heart clenched. Everyone knowing was like little stabs in my heart.

I couldn't breathe.

I tried to remind myself that peace came from within, right? I'd never let Jeremy know he'd hurt me. I'd never be like my mom.

I hung the dress on a hanger and zipped it in the bag as Michael said, "We can stream the whole thing, so you can share the high def video."

I'd call tomorrow in the group chat as I'd planned, though Jeremy had already told them with one video. I nodded at him and said, "Okay. I'll call them later."

Jeremy and Michael were dressed, and I was still in my white slip.

I finished packing the dress and went for the package as Michael said, "Time is speeding up. Right now, we have a flight to Tulsa as I have a game tonight."

Time flew. I opened the white cotton dress and said, "I'll finish fast. We can skip lunch as I'm not hungry."

He confirmed something on his phone as it beeped and he said, "No problem."

I took my pins out of my hair and let my hair fall behind my ears and neck. Then I gave them both a thumbs-up and said, "Done."

He kissed my palm as he directed us out of the room and said, "Sorry about the speed of the day."

We ran toward the limo where the driver already loaded our bags, as I said, "It's fun to have all these places to be."

Once we were heading back to the airport, that we could already see without touching the champagne, I caught my breath.

Michael then said, "I had my maid clean up the guest room for Jeremy tonight."

Weddings seemed dreamlike, but this rushing around was fun. As the limo pulled into the spot, Jeremy said, "Must be nice to have a maid. Are we rich now?"

Michael checked us in first-class where there was no waiting. Then he said, "We have money to pay for what you need."

As we went to security, we were practically waved through as Jeremy said, "How about a nice car when I'm old enough?"

A small chuckle came out of my mouth and I shook my head. Money wasn't a reason to agree to everything. My son's bargaining was funny, but I'd not laugh, as Michael said, "I think we can handle that."

Once we passed the guards, and I had my dress in my hand, I said, "We're not talking about money anymore Jeremy, and don't bring the topic up with your friends."

"Yes, Mom," Jeremy said, then took his seat in first-class where a flight attendant was getting him a juice.

I put my seat belt on.

I'd have to watch to make sure he didn't get too spoiled.

The plane finished loading and he said, "In Tulsa, I need to go to practice, but you two can meet me, and tomorrow I have the day off so we can celebrate without having to board planes."

Good. Life was great. We held hands and the flight was fast.

I went into a dream state for a while as I stared at my ring. The princess cut was a few carats from the size and weight of it. Honestly, I never expected to marry or have a ring of my own. I wasn't sure what to say. I blanked out for a while. I knew we landed, and I knew we were safe in a car Michael drove. But I'd stopped believing in ever getting married. This moment seemed unreal.

My bubble burst when we drove into a large gated estate home and Michael frowned as he said, "This is my…house. Georgie, Jeremy, it seems my parents came unexpectedly today."

Parents. I had pins and needles in my arms now, but I swallowed and said like everything was under control, "It will be nice to meet them."

He parked his car in his garage that had three more cars.

I glanced around to see everything and noticed the cowboy hat on the coat rack near the door. We stepped into a foyer, and an older woman with curly hair and a man who was a slightly balding version of Michael, stood. His mother wrapped her arms around me and said, "So this is the girl you've been pining for."

"Mom!" Michael said and sounded a little like Jeremy in that moment, which made me laugh.

If my son grew into Michael, we'd need that gate to keep out the girls. His mother let me go but hugged Michael as she said, "It's true. My son has been talking about you for years."

Sweet. I checked my dress didn't have a wrinkle and said, "Well, that's nice to hear." And then I offered my hand to shake his father's hand. "Nice to meet you. I'm Georgiana."

Michael held my waist and said, "Georgie, this is my mom, Sarah, and my dad, Tom."

The family resemblance was uncanny with that strong chin of theirs. I shook their hands and said, "Nice to meet you both. How was the wedding?"

They knew. My face heated. "Beautiful."

Michael put his hands on Jeremy's shoulders while he said, "Mom. Dad. This is your grandson, Jeremy."

My son held his hand out to shake when he said, "Nice to meet you."

Sarah went down on one knee and threw her arms wide open as she said, "Come here. We're huggers."

My son hugged her, and everyone seemed complete. Sarah then glanced at me and said, "Your dad wants to know if we can treat Jeremy to an ice cream."

I nodded to Michael that it was fine, then my lips pressed together. My mother would have done exactly this.

"That sounds fun," Jeremy said. "Michael promised me ice cream in Vegas, but we ran out of time."

"We can make up for that. All the men in the family love chocolate syrup on ice cream," Tom said and patted my son, who had his profile, on the back as he added, "We'll be back in two hours, then we can all go to the game together."

The nose was clearly a family hand me down from Tom to Michael and now to Jeremy as I glanced at the profiles. We walked them to the front door and Michael asked his parents, "How long do you plan on staying in town?"

His mother said, "Our tickets are for tomorrow. We're staying in a hotel."

So, we were to be alone. I sucked my breath as that was rude. This house seemed huge, unless the extra rooms were all game rooms, baseball memorials, libraries, indoor pools, tennis courts, or something. I hadn't inspected to know, I met Michael's gaze and his face was red as he said, "You don't have to."

His mother said 'pfft' and shook her head. "We're giving you both space. It's your wedding night! Maybe tomorrow, if Jeremy likes us and the ice cream, then you can let us have breakfast with our grandson."

Jeremy gave a thumbs-up as he headed into the car with them. There was a booster seat in the back they must have rented.

"I'm happy to have grandparents," Jeremy said.

"See you soon," I said and waved them off.

The rented SUV drove off, but we stood on the driveway until the car was out of sight. Michael pressed his hand on my lower back. "We're alone."

I walked beside him and as the door closed, I laughed and said, "It is our wedding day."

His blue eyes had a twinkle in them as he glanced up and down my body. My skin was alive and well aware of him, though I ignored the feeling. "True, and you are wearing too many clothes."

Well, my instinct had been right on, but I shrugged like I didn't understand and said, "My dress is all packed up. Vegas was pretty fun. I'd never been there."

He swept his hands on my sides and unzipped me a little. "Don't distract me, Georgie."

I batted my eyes a little too much and asked, "What do you want?"

He guided me to walk backward into another room in his house, as my dress draped open on the side, as he said, "You…me…one time before they get back. Two hours is not that long, and I have a game tonight."

I nodded and stopped pretending. I wanted this, too. Michael and I made sense physically as he was the only one that made me see the stars. "So, where is your bedroom?"

He tugged the shoulders of the dress to get it to fall off. "Oh, you and I aren't getting that far. My couch is near the fireplace."

I laughed and decided not to play coy anymore. I tugged on his t-shirt and he helped peel it off as I asked, "So, that's what you want?"

"I just want you. My mother told you the truth."

My heart pounded in my chest and goose-bumps grew on my arms. Michael Irons must have had his pick of women. Yet he was here, with me, married like we were in love. I swallowed and hoped I sounded light as I said, "That you missed me."

He then pressed his forehead to mine and didn't move. "That I didn't want another woman in seven years, so I'm rearing to go again with you."

This was mutual sexual hunger. I held him tighter and closed my eyes as our breaths mixed between us. "I didn't want another man to be honest. The one guy who kissed me was boring and I never even invited that."

His face grew grave like I'd just told him someone beat me as he asked, "Who was it?"

I shook my head and said, "A widower with six children. He was just so happy some Church women babysat and gave him the night off."

"I'm still jealous." Michael unzipped his pants and my heart beat faster as he asked, "Who watched Jeremy?"

"Olivia," I said as his pants dropped to the ground.

He tugged my bra free and then stared at me once it fell.

His perusal made me hot as he said, "Now, this is how I like to remember you."

He then kissed me, and steam rose through me. His hand pressed against my thigh, including the new, cold, gold ring he wore. I couldn't think straight as he led me to the couch as I asked, "Will the ring interfere with your game?"

"None of the other guys complain. I'll let you

know," he said, then the last bit of our clothes came off as he tasted me everywhere and sent me straight into a heavenly orbit where all that mattered was more of this. Us together, forever.

This was ideal. I'd never wanted love and, in time, I'd figure out how to be calm near him. Then, we'd be perfect. For now, I had this, with Michael.

Chapter 10

Michael

The game went fast and then it was time to head home, to the wife I'd had to leave in our bed.

Granted, I'd seen her with my parents and son in the stands, but I'd had no chance to see them.

Georgie's body still rocked my body like gravity meeting a meteor. She burned through me, but I needed every part of her for more.

I'd probably never be satisfied, and I didn't care. She was my wife now.

We'd won, and I raced out the second I could.

The moon was high in the sky when I drove into my house and joined Georgie in bed.

I dozed the second I curled beside Georgie and she smelled sweeter than roses to me.

I woke up alone. I cleaned up and walked down the stairs fast, to see my family. Jeremy was sitting on the couch. My father came out of the kitchen and said, "Georgie said it was okay if I took Jeremy to go get a hot chocolate in town."

"Yeah?"

"Your mother and I will be gone an hour, if it's all right with you."

"Georgie said it was fine, so have fun."

Jeremy hopped out of his seat and followed my dad to the door. Clearly, my father was doing his charming old man bit.

He did that well at first, though no one but me ever knew how driven he actually was.

I embodied his dreams, but I waved them hello and kept my mouth shut. I needed to see my wife, but my mom was near the coffee that smelled earthy and perfect. She said, "We'll be back soon."

"I'm looking forward to seeing more of you." Georgie came out of the bathroom and her lips curled higher the second she noticed me.

My mother hugged me and Georgie, then went out to join my dad and Jeremy.

I didn't blink. Georgie made the room shine, but she headed toward the counter and my mom, still wearing pink pajama bottoms and a Sooners t-shirt that went off her shoulder.

My stomach churned. I was hungry right now… I followed her to the kitchen to the smell of coffee. I made glasses and she finished making toast, and I asked once the machine was heating up the milk, "You're okay if I ask them to stay the full weekend?"

She nodded and took out a mango, cutting it as she said, "It's good. They were fun last night at the game. Your father talked about your childhood and how he really worked with you to get your stats up and Jeremy is enjoying spending time with them more than I'd ever imagined."

She'd gotten the highlights of my childhood then, though she'd missed out on how not even rainstorms had stopped our nightly training for me to have what my father hadn't. I was sure Dad made it all sound fun, but I grabbed some brie cheese from the fridge and a mix of almonds and walnuts as I said, "He pushed me to the pros."

"I could tell from his intensity and excitement for you."

Maybe he'd explain how his dad had kept him well past nightfall in practice when most kids went home and did their homework. I handed her a bowl for her mangoes and took our offerings to the table. "He made it to the farm for a few years but never moved up to the minors or pros."

The toast popped and she took it out, joining me as she placed it all in the middle of the table. "He told me and he swore you'd have that opportunity that he wasted."

Now, that sounded like his promise or threat if I whined about practice. However, when I gave up for a few weeks in high school, I'd realized I wanted baseball as my career.

I took a piece of toast and said, "I'm good at the game I love. Jeremy can choose my sport, another one, or a future doing whatever he wants."

We both added brie to our toast as she said, "Glad to hear…" The ring in the air caught her off guard and she jumped up and found where we had charged our phones last night. She took hers and said, "My sisters are calling. Phone conference time."

"Get it," I said, as last night she'd intended to call them today, so I gave her a thumbs-up.

Maybe after she talked to them and we ate, we'd have time for another round before Jeremy and my parents returned. They'd been good to give us some time alone, and I'd wait. Georgie'd be happier after talking to her family.

She choked down her bread fast and said, "Thanks."

A moment later, she answered, but put her call on speaker, as her sister said, "So you're married?"

She added some walnuts and almonds on her cheese and said, "Olivia, Michael and I both want the best for Jeremy."

"You and Stephanie were both so adamant about never marrying. Now she's engaged and you're married. Aren't you afraid?"

Georgie put her food down and met my gaze. Her brown eyes had some deep emotion in them I didn't quite understand. "No. I'm never going to give up on life if something happens to Michael. We talked about it."

Interesting. I had no siblings and had zero idea how women talked to each other. My friends and I would be swearing and avoiding the direct topic to a common dominator or just telling directly "not your business". Her sister then said, "Well that's good, as long as you're happy."

"I am."

Good. I bit another bite of my toast and then her sister asked her, "How do you know you won't turn into Mom?"

My heart slowed as my ears listened closer. Georgie had mentioned her mother and how she had wanted to die. How deep was that fear? It related to how long it might take for me to tell her I loved her? This wasn't just sex for me. My stomach twisted at the idea she married me only for money when I was falling hard for her and probably had years ago.

Georgie tugged her ear and met my gaze as she asked, "Why are you asking?"

For a second, I didn't move, like she'd read my mind, but Olivia asked her, "I want to know how I can ever trust myself like you and Stephanie clearly have."

If Olivia was my sister, I'd tell her not to take what happens to others as something destined. What happened to our parents doesn't have to be the truth for us. My parents were friends, but Georgie and I were more. She'd see that in time.

My fortune had come from hard work and laser focus on what I wanted.

However, Georgie lowered her lashes and her cheeks blushed as she said, "Well, Michael and I talked about it, and I hope whoever you might think about marrying supports you being independent."

More than that. Georgie and I were good together because we weren't sacrificing who we were or what we wanted. She wanted to be home and to take care of our son. I'd enhance that life-style. Life was good.

Olivia asked Georgie, "But how do I trust myself?"

She took my hand and her brown eyes were full of trust as she nodded at me and smiled, "To be honest, Jeremy is my reason I can take this chance. He deserves to have a good dad, like we had."

I'd honor that. Our boy, not me, was a reason to pick up and take the best contract. Olivia said, "I don't have a son that needs me."

Now I understood her sister was clearly the needy type. Maybe that's why she was a teacher, a job I could never do. "Olivia, it will be okay. When you meet the guy you trust, you'll know."

"I guess," her sister mumbled.

Trust was a good start, but in time, I'd want more. Georgie let my hand go and fixed more cheese on her bread as she said, "Look, I have to go."

The women said goodbye and I jumped up to get our coffees. "Your sister takes that pact seriously."

She put her phone away as I slipped her a coffee.

"Her boyfriend broke up with her right before Dad died. She was devastated and never got over it. When we made our pact, she'd thought that was why he'd left her or something like that."

"That doesn't' make sense."

"Love doesn't make sense. I'm glad we married for more practical reasons."

Right. She needed time. She took a sip and sighed a little contentment as I prompted so she'd tell me more. "You were talking about support and taking chances."

She took the last long sip of her coffee, then said, "When my mother died, it was because she gave up on life after my father. She never made a choice and preferred to be in the shadow until the very end. We talked about how you don't want my love like that."

Interesting. I hadn't expected the intensity of how the words of love poured out of me. "I'd want my mom to live if something happened to my dad."

"Good." She nodded and then ate her toast.

"And for you to tell me what you think."

We both ate a few minutes. As we finished, I helped pick up the plates and said, "To be honest, my dad was intense."

She helped me but then refilled our coffee cups and said, "My dad was the heart of the family. Losing him meant we lost who checked up on us, who took us to the doctor and came to school to get us."

I washed the dishes. In my family, that was absolutely my mom. "Your mom didn't even keep doctor appointments for you?"

She joined me to dry the dishes and said, "My mom was good but she…she survived tragedy in her younger years. Abuse, and sometimes she just ghosted on us when we had a crisis."

"The exact opposite of my childhood. My mother was the one that kissed all my bruises and took me to school while Dad worked." I couldn't imagine life without her near her when I was young. I squeezed Georgie's hand and said, "That's hard."

She shrugged. "In her way, she tried, but she honestly didn't know how to live without my father."

I pivoted closer to her. "You'll never be like that."

She sucked in her lower lip, as I'd noticed was her habit, then let it out as she asked, "How are you sure?"

"Because it's not about loving someone." I guided her toward the coffee she'd poured and took one as I said, "It's about loving and trusting yourself, which you seem to do, Georgie."

She held the cup closer to her face. "I tend to isolate myself, which is very much like my mother."

That wasn't quite true. Georgie took a moment to analyze, but I didn't think she'd want to argue right now. I motioned toward our chairs to have our second cup as I said, "Not telling someone your business is not the same thing."

"I hope you're right." She sipped when she sat.

She seemed quiet, but she just made me more sure that she was perfect for me. I winked and joked, "The marriage will work out better if you think I'm always right, Georgie."

We both drank our coffees though she said, "Your house here in Tulsa is much bigger than my house."

Good. The conversation was where I needed it. I put my cup down and laid my hands on the table as I said, "And the schools are excellent, if I stay with the Sooners."

She sipped her coffee again and then once she finished said, "Having your address in chaos has to be hard."

This conversation was important. I nodded. "Even if the Pirates come through on some amazing last-minute offer, I'd want to take Jeremy to whatever the best schools are and the nicest area to live."

"I'm open to change." She put her cup down. "I want what's best for Jeremy."

"That we'll do." I finished my own cup and then asked, "Even if we end up getting anything from Boston to LA or any city with a major league?"

She reached out and held my wrists as she said, "I said yes to our marriage, and if my sister Stephanie can pick up and live in London, I can be open as long as we keep Jeremy's life and education stable."

I stood and held out my hands for her as I said, "Good, now let's celebrate naked before my parents get back with Jeremy."

Her face grew warmer as she joined me, leaving our cups as they were. This time, I held her as we walked upstairs as I could pretend to be a gentleman with her. On the steps, she asked, "Michael?"

"Yeah?" I asked and hoped she didn't change anything now.

She bumped into me and said, "I'm happy with you."

Life was exactly right, then. We made it to the

top step and I said, "Good because I'm happy I get to have you, forever, now."

As we neared the bedroom door, I kissed her. I didn't want this to ever end. Georgie here gave me everything I'd ever wanted in life.

Chapter 11

Georgie

Michael and I had a perfect plan. If we stayed as we were and never fell in love, then I wasn't in danger. I'd figure out how to bring peace back in my life. We worked as a team, where we talked about our wants and desires and figured out how to support each other.

This was for the best.

I cleaned myself up and flounced down the stairs when I heard the doorbell.

Jeremy was probably back now, but as I neared the door in my jeans and red t-shirt, I saw Michael open the door to a slicked back, grey-haired man. Michael shook his hand and said, "Phil."

I walked over, happy I knew it was his agent, and nothing was changing as Phil said, "Michael, I hope it's okay I came over?"

"Come in," he said but then the garage door opened, and Jeremy was in the backseat of the rented minivan. We walked inside and Michael told them as they joined us, "Mom, Dad, Jeremy, Georgie this is my agent, Phil. We're gonna talk about my offers."

His mother headed into the kitchen immediately. Did I go with her? I stilled as his father asked, "Do you want us to go somewhere?"

Michael shook his head and said, "No. Dad you got me my shot. Georgie and Jeremy have a stake in the future too. I'd like for us to all talk about this."

His mother popped her head in from the kitchen and said, "I'll change our tickets to later in the day if you want our opinion."

Seriously? She didn't want to be part of the conversation over her son's future? My pulse raced as that was often what my own mother did as Michael asked me, "Would that be okay, Georgie?"

Sarah stared at me. My skin had pins and needles. This was exactly how my family had worked, where my mom just left the important discussions, but I smiled at her and said, "I'd love for you to stay. We've not had enough time to talk."

Sarah tapped the wall and headed out of the room. "I'll change them then."

Her leaving the room was exactly what my mom would have done.

My spine tingled. She had tickets to change so I wasn't being rational. Michael led the rest of us to his formal dining room. The room had a table for twelve and the oak was polished and the white cushioned seats were spotless.

Did he use this room often? My skin had cold spikes over it. It's not like I'd known Michael for long. We all took seats and Phil took out papers from his briefcase as Michael asked, "So Phil, what are the options?"

He took out the first file and handed it over. "The Sooners upped their offer after your recent performances and the playoff potential."

Seven years at twenty-five million. The number was close to what Michael wanted, and I glanced around the huge estate. This could be transformed to be more kid friendly and elegant. His house felt barely lived in. "Your house here is nice."

"What else?" Michael pushed it toward his father and signaled for another paper.

Phil handed another folder over and said,

"Boston has a strong offer and the benefits are good."

Twenty-three million for eight years. Massachusetts didn't seem that different than Pittsburgh, but Michael wrote on the side "high taxes". I read it and so did his agent as he said, "This sounds right. What else?"

Smart. Take-home pay mattered, and Phil said, "New York has the highest offer but after taxes it's almost equal to the Sooners."

New York's offer was twenty-nine a year for eight years.

My stomach tightened as I'd been physically sick the only time I'd been in Manhattan. My son needed security and I trembled under the table. Sarah returned with glasses of water on a tray and started serving everyone. I asked, "What about Pittsburgh?"

Did Michael expect me to serve like this? Quietly not having an opinion but there to kiss Jeremy's bruises?

Phil said to Jeremy, "Their offer wasn't serious before. I sent the personalized request but so far, no answer."

My son's face fell to his chin and he swung his legs. I asked, "Jeremy, what are your thoughts?"

Jeremy met my gaze and didn't' blink at all when he said, "I just hate leaving my friends."

At six, he probably was but, in time, he'd make new friends. "We have to go back and visit all the time. All your aunts are there."

His father then asked, "Anything from Texas?"

Wait. Texas? My mind was spinning. Sarah now brought in a small tray of crackers and cheese for the table as Phil said, "The Rangers have a decent starting point. I could continue negotiations if I can say you're serious."

Twenty-two million for eight years. Michael asked, "Why, Dad?"

He nodded and said, "I always liked the Rangers organization and Texas."

Something unsaid was happening between the men, but he showed me the paper and wrote low taxes as he said, "Georgie, what do you think?"

Well low taxes meant more take-home pay and more available for savings. And the Sooners might be what he wanted, and this house was nice. I nodded, but honestly, my thoughts rushed and I wasn't sure. I was open to both places. Honestly, I'd never been to Texas but the houses there on TV always seemed big, so I said, "I think...loyalty is a good thing. I'd say the Sooners should be number one. I think Texas is better than New York for us if I'm being honest."

His gaze narrowed and my heart raced like I'd said the wrong thing when he asked, "Why?"

My skin was jumpy. "Houses are big and less taxes sound nice."

"Talk to the Rangers." Michael nodded and told Phil, "And if Pittsburgh doesn't bring an offer, our third major franchise should be New York."

My heart sank. I'd been to Manhattan and that wasn't my cup of tea when I asked, "Why New York?"

"If I'm selling out my team for money, New York generally has the most and I look good in pinstripes."

Team? He hadn't sounded loyal to the Sooners. Maybe he'd always wanted to be on that team, but my stomach twisted. My tongue was thick in my throat, but words didn't form. Tight spaces full of people all the time was a horrible way to live. I lowered my head. I wanted to scream, cry, but all I said was, "I never wanted to live in New York."

He pressed my lower back. "It's closer to Pittsburgh to see your family."

I'd not dash his dream, though the idea of New York made my body tense as I said, "That's true. It's fine."

Fine was the exact opposite of true. I really was turning into my mom now.

Boston and New York just weren't my style. I preferred to spread out with a big house like this, the plains of Texas or even a mountain view and asked, "What about Colorado? What was their offer like?"

Phil shook his head but took out another file as he said, "Lower, but St. Louis was extremely competitive."

Ten years but twenty-one million. The years were what Michael wanted and I nodded and said, "I'm fine with St. Louis."

Phil asked, "Then I should focus on the Sooners, the Rangers, and St. Louis?"

"Yes," Sarah said to summarize.

"How about Houston?" Tom asked.

Phil ruffled his briefcase and said, "Their offer was competitive too. Would that be a good finalist?"

Nine years at twenty million.

Michael wanted thirty for a ten-year contract. Phil had to know the goal if he was talking competitive, so I said, "Yeah. Any other major team with a high offer?"

"We discussed the offers over twenty now." And he showed his paper with the notes as he said,

"After taxes you walk away with more money with these teams."

Michael stood and shook hands. "I trust you Phil. Bring the final number to thirty for ten and we're going to that team as a done deal. Nothing has changed."

"Got it," he said, and Michael walked him to the door.

Jeremy asked me, "So we're definitely moving, Mom?"

He'd be fine. My stomach twisted again at the thought of New York. "It will be an adventure."

"I guess," he said, though he had little enthusiasm.

Michael returned and he met his gaze. "I…I'm okay if we do."

I wasn't. My insides burned, but I forced my cheeks to lift when I said, "Good. Me, too."

His father, Tom said. "Let's celebrate before we all head home."

Sarah jumped up, collecting the waters as Michael asked, "What do you have in mind?"

I watched her closely. Michael had said she'd been the one who'd bandaged his bruises, but Sarah silently went about cleaning up as Tom said, "I'll grill us some steaks. You and your pretty wife get the beer and wine. And tonight, your mom and I head back to Florida."

I'd had my chance to speak and chosen to be silent. I swallowed. If Michael took the job, somehow, I'd have to find the words. Calmness and peace would never be my life, not in that huge city. My heart raced at the thought of being stuck there. I couldn't turn into my mother like this and disappear. I'd behaved just like her right now. My mind raced. Would I transform into my mother if I just accepted this silently?

Michael asked his father, "If we move to Texas, it's warm there, Dad."

Warm was good. I took a deep breath. Nothing was set in stone yet.

Tom gave him a thumbs-up and said, "I always liked it there."

"So you'll move?" Michael asked.

Guess I knew where he wanted, and it wasn't crazy New York. My stomach relaxed as I went to help Sarah carry the cheese plate as Michael said, "It will be good to have our family close and to get to know Jeremy."

"I'd like that, Mom," Jeremy said and tapped Michael's father like they were already bonded.

I put the tray back in the huge refrigerator. Michael followed me and picked up his keys.

He beamed at me like he was so close to every-thing he wanted. "Text Phil. Tell him we want the Texas teams as the number one and two choices."

His gaze met mine as he asked, "You're sure?"

This could all destroy me. He waved for me to join him and then opened the garage door for me, grabbed his cowboy hat, and tossed it on his head. "Yeah. Let's get in the car to get the beers." Jeremy came out and Michael then asked him, "You want to stay or come, Jeremy?"

"I'll stay. See you soon." He waved and then joined his grandmother at the sink to help with the dishes.

I glanced back one more time and followed Michael out. I wasn't losing myself because I loved Michael.

The thought stilled me until he opened my door.

I jumped in and hoped I could, somehow, will words out of my mouth. This silence that overcame me, paralyzed me.

Love was bad when it froze my voice. Today couldn't be the start of that horrible fate. I couldn't let it destroy me.

Chapter 12

Michael

New York before taxes was the best offer and the closest to my goals. Without one word I understood Georgie wasn't on board with the plan. My hair stood on its ends at the thought that I could lose out on my thirty million a year for ten years plan because Georgie didn't want New York.

She hadn't said too much negative, but her lack of color when the numbers had been read was a hint. My spine had tightened.

I refused to be loyal to any team, but history showed they cared about their team and paid their players. At twenty-nine million, they were inches from my finish line.

Boston wasn't too far behind my final number either. Money meant I'd provide for my son and have a stronger portfolio for his children's children. Investments require security and swinging my bat for the highest price guaranteed this. I'd spent my life preparing for this moment. I'd be stupid if I had to give up on the big boys with the large checks…

Rather than discuss it, Georgie kept quiet beside me on a small trip to the grocery and liquor store.

Dad hadn't asked for more steaks or potatoes, but I knew my dad. I'd grab corn on the cob, fresh steaks, not frozen, and a bag of potatoes.

The barbeque would be awesome as my dad made the best grill chef. My phone beeped as we made it closer to the store, and I parked when I read his message. "Get extra in case anyone wants seconds."

She sucked in her top lip and then let it out. "Sounds good. I've not had steak on a grill in a long time."

"I texted my dad 'no problem'," I said, and quickly sent the text. Then I opened my door. I went to her side, but she'd already let herself out.

"He'll want Corona, but I like Guinness."

She linked her arm with mine and said, "And your mom?"

I told her as we headed into the liquor store and added our items to the maroon cart. "White wine."

She read a few labels and I pointed to one I knew Mom liked.

"Okay," she said.

We had three drinks in the cart now. "And you?"

She avoided my gaze. "I'm not picky."

I pointed around the store and said, "The world is your oyster. Get what you want, including non-alcoholic if that's your preference."

Her face turned bright red as she blushed and squared her shoulders. "I want…to not be dragged to New York."

Goosebumps grew on my arm like she didn't support my choice anymore, though she hadn't said officially. We headed to the cashier. "What's wrong with New York? It's a fun place."

I gave the clerk my card and turned from Georgie for a moment. Her frown was clear from her profile, but once we paid and had our bags Georgie said, "I've been to Manhattan, and I needed a vacation to get over it."

I carried our bags to the trunk of the car and ignored how my heart raced as I said, "We don't have to live in Manhattan."

She scoffed and raised her eyebrow. "You want

the best of the best, and I can't change who I am to live in New York. I wouldn't know how."

I closed the door and took a deep breath. No need to stress as it was only a possibility as this point. "Texas would make my dad happy as well as you."

She walked with me to the grocery store without a glance, but said with a frown, "I might hate it there too. I've never been."

I needed her and baseball to make my life whole. This was what we'd agreed to when I'd told her my plans.

I ignored how my skin prickled on my arms and asked her instead, "Where have you been?"

We went to the vegetables and found the corn on the cob as she said, "Pittsburgh, Orlando once, and the Bahamas."

I'd seen all fifty states at this point in my life and half of Europe on vacations. We grabbed the potatoes next as I asked, "That's it?"

She shrugged and said, "I've not been to London to see my sister. I've never really traveled, but she's expecting us at the wedding."

If our lives didn't mesh, we were both in trouble. "Are you against travel?"

"No," she said as we headed to the butcher section. "I want Jeremy to see more of the world, but I've been worried about spending the money. And the holiday season is usually expensive."

I picked up six prime cuts and tossed them in the basket. "We'll get passports and go to your sister's wedding as a family."

Her face brightened like I'd thrown her a life-line. "That would be great."

I pushed the cart forward and tried to match her glee. "Christmas in London, sounds like a movie title."

She gently pushed into my side and said, "And thank you for listening to me about New York."

Only if they weren't the best offer. Otherwise, we'd have our first serious argument. We paid at the self-checkout. "If they up their offer and it's the most after taxes though, we'll need to talk about it again."

She crossed her arms and stared at me as I paid with my card. As we finished and I grabbed the bags, she asked, "Just talk? Or are you going to sign and ask me later?"

I knew she had more to say. My own face heated. Maybe that had been my plan. I hadn't visualized it. "You said you were okay with me going after the money."

"I am." She walked with me as she then said, "I'm just not okay with how close everyone lives in

New York. My two-story house, with three bedrooms and a basement and attic sometimes feels small for me, and it's just two people."

Score one for Georgie. Space wasn't known in Manhattan, and I hadn't researched commute options with bigger homes. If that was the best option in the end, we'd figure something out. Cramped wasn't an image I saw as optimal either for raising our son. "I promise to talk to you before signing anything."

I opened her door and she hopped in the passenger seat as she said, "That's good."

I packed our purchases behind me and then joined her. I held the key in my hand but didn't turn it on yet as I said, "One more thing."

Her eyes widened as she stared at me. "Yeah?"

I'd never push Jeremy the way I was to the point of exhaustion, though now I had the benefits of those nights in the palm of my hand. "My parents-"

"Your mom and dad are great," she interrupted.

For now. My father was intense. She had no idea, but I pressed the button for ignition and started our drive home. "They are when they want to make an impression and they want Jeremy to like them."

She fixed her seat belt. "It's helping with our son wanting to move."

"I can have them fly out more often," I said then, especially if New York was the answer. They'd stay in Florida but visit and help with my son when I couldn't be there.

She turned on the radio and bobbed her head to the music. "Jeremy likes them, but I can't promise to ever be like your mom and not voice my opinion."

I turned off the radio as my gut said this was important. "Like how?"

She pressed her lips together and then finally said, "She was serving while her family discussed."

"She said what she wanted and talked to the airline. Besides, my contract doesn't change her life much," I said as an immediate defense of her running to the kitchen. I'd learned as a boy not to question her and then added, "She's a retired teacher. If I ever needed help figuring out what to do for almost anything other than baseball, she'd be my go-to call."

Georgie jerked her head and her eyes went cold as she yelled like I'd said something important. "She was a teacher?"

This wasn't about my mom. My skin was

prickly as I couldn't make the connection and said, "Yeah, like your sister."

"I didn't know that." She pushed her hands together like in prayer and slumped her head down. "My mom didn't work. She just stayed home and cooked six or more different meals, always giving us whatever we wanted."

A tear raced down her cheek. She didn't wipe at it and stayed absolutely still.

I reached out my hand and said, "It's okay. We don't know everything about each other yet."

She took it and squeezed it as we made our way back to our home. "But I can't sit by while you make a decision for all three of us."

I let her go and pressed the button for the garage. "I won't ask you to. I need you and baseball to make my life complete."

She smiled and unbuttoned herself. "And you have that."

I turned off the engine and reached for my door. "Then let's get back inside."

She got out, but as we went to unload everything she reached for the bags. "I'll have white wine with your mom as that's often my favorite. It's why I didn't ask for anything."

The more I knew her, the better we'd all be. I'd

also ensure none of us ever stressed about money again, and the contract secured our future.

I said quickly, "Next time, make your decision faster?"

She didn't move and lowered her lashes as she said, "I'm still getting used to speaking up. I haven't had to talk to anyone about my choices since I've grown up. Give me time."

If that was all this was, we had everything we needed. I swallowed and said, "You have all the time in the world, Georgie. I'm seriously in love with you."

I hadn't meant to let that slip. The words had fallen out of my mouth.

She let the bags in her hand fall back in the trunk and stared at me with glassy eyes and a white face as she asked, "You are?"

"I fucking love you," I said, and grabbed her to hold her. No denying the truth now.

She curled into me and pressed her lips up to me as she whispered, "I love you too, and it scares me."

Everything else had to work out then. We were together. Money wasn't everything, right?

Chapter 13

Georgie

The barbeque in the backyard now had that familiar singe in the air I'd not heard in years.

Michael left his sexy cowboy hat in the garage on his keyring, which only made me giggle to myself.

There was something fun about steaks on a grill, buttered corn roasting, and mashed potatoes covered in aluminum all mixed together that made my mouth water.

But it wasn't ready yet. I finished handing out the drinks to everyone, including myself, when my phone rang. I put my glass down and walked back in the house as I answered my sister in London. "Stephanie, hi."

"You've not called me or anyone except Olivia and the others."

I closed the door as I said, "Technically, Olivia called me, and I knew someone would have filled you in."

"I watched your wedding video," Stephanie said.

I froze and wondered how in the world to love when dying for it was in my genes. Maybe that was foolish, but I asked, "Yeah?"

Stephanie said, "You were beautiful."

If anyone had the answer, it was Stephanie. I checked I was alone and stared at everyone outside near the grill as I said, "Thanks. It was a last-minute decision."

She laughed. "I'm a total believer in happily-ever-afters and love. You, Jeremy, and your Michael are now on my guest list. So was my decision to marry Charles and move to London. I couldn't have explained that to you."

When I was driving Stephanie to the airport for her vacation, I hadn't thought that was the last time I'd see my sister. I ignored how my heart grew faster and turned away from the window so I could be totally alone as I asked, "Can I ask a quick question before I say I have to go?"

Stephanie snapped her fingers. "Go for it."

I tugged my ear and then decided it was time to ask, "How did you trust yourself to love your fiancée after Mom…"

"After Mom gave up like she did and stopped even communicating?" Stephanie supplied the question.

My cheeks heated. All six of us and our cousins had held hands and buried her with our dad, and sworn that day, we'd be there for each other and to never be like her. Then my entire family had been there for me when I'd needed help for the weeks after Jeremy was born. I'd had cousins flying in from all over the country to pitch in, like we were children again. I couldn't have done it without them, but I nodded and said, "Yeah."

I hugged my waist while Stephanie said, "I had to figure out my life mattered too and I wasn't going to turn into her because love makes me and Charles better, not worse."

Without children, maybe trust was easier. I'd been in love with Michael since we met really, but only now, I had to face facts. Love didn't always come with an exit clause, and I glanced at my feet as I said, "Guess you don't have a son to worry about."

Stephanie quietly said, "That's more of a reason to know you won't just give up if something bad happens."

Yet that hadn't been enough for Mom when I'd told her I was pregnant and needed her help. Why would faith work with Michael? He had the world waiting for him to make a decision and I wasn't ready to be on display. I closed my eyes to get my trembling skin under control as I said, "I don't know."

"My advice." Stephanie took a second and then said, "If you love him, then trust your new husband and trust yourself. You've needed to let loose for a long time."

Goosebumps grew on my arm. I needed to protect myself and protect Jeremy to ensure I'd be there forever for him. This wasn't about relaxing. It was impossible near him. I loved Michael, but that had to be second. I couldn't turn weak now. Stephanie didn't have this worry. She'd never understand as she chased after whatever whim she had. "I have to go."

We said goodbye, and I glanced out the window. Jeremy was playing catch with Michael who was showing him posture.

I could watch this all day. Jeremy needed Michael. A good dad was important to a family and so was a strong mother.

I needed to protect my heart from ever clinging so much to Michael that I lost my will to live.

It shouldn't be too hard.

I turned my phone off so no one else could call me and walked outside with a strut to my step.

Michael and Jeremy stopped. Sarah helped Tom put the food on plates and Michael rushed over and kissed my forehead. "Where were you?"

"My sister called from London."

"How is she?"

"It's late in London, but she's good."

Michael walked us over and his mother must have given him a look as he said, "Georgie has five sisters, Mom."

I took a seat next to her and poured the wine for us as Michael passed his father a beer. Jeremy took a water on his own and we all sat as Sarah said, "That's great. I always wanted a daughter. It must have been great growing up with all those people around you."

"My parents pretty much adopted all our cousins at some point in their lives, so our house was always full."

"A house full of love. That sounds lovely."

Tom led us in a short prayer. It was good to have sisters and male cousins with cars when my mom wasn't available to help me. Michael had his parents still, so he'd not quite understand.

As we finished, we started eating, though I'd just cut my meat as I said, "When my parents died, I became the makeshift mom of the group as I'm the oldest woman. Everyone in the family usually calls me. Plus, with raising Jeremy, I always had to make good decisions that help everyone lead their best life."

I took a bite and the steak was perfect.

No restaurant quite got the mix of fire and meat right, but Tom had a gift. I gave a thumbs-up. Sarah asked me, "What about you? What is it you want now that you have Michael?"

I finished my bite and it took a minute. I then raised my eyebrow and asked, "What do I want?"

Sarah held her napkin in her hand and had her elbows on the table as she smiled at me and said, "Yes, sweetie. You have the ability to do anything in the world you desire."

At least we weren't prim and proper like the private schools had taught me. I glanced at my plate and said, "I just want my son to have the best opportunities he can have."

Tom then said, "Jeremy was telling us he plays little league."

Pushing Jeremy if he didn't want it would just make us all miserable. "The pressure of being Michael Irons' son, now that it's known, has to be hard to live up to."

Tom shrugged and said, "Not impossible if that's what he wants."

"True," Michael said but then patted my knee. "That's Jeremy's choice."

Agreement was good. This was easier than deciding where we lived for a decade.

Sarah ensured we all had napkins and then settled. "Other than marrying my son, tell us more about yourself. What did you major in college, dear?"

I finished my next bite and remembered care-free college. Time had flown and the memories were almost like another life. "I was finance major, though I never used it much."

Tom asked, "Why not?"

Right. For the second time in days, I'd actually answer with the truth. I normally avoided it, but the last thing I needed were Michael's parents to think I needed Michael's money, and that I was some gold-digger. I folded my hands. "I was working but then my parents died, and I had an inheritance and a newborn."

His mother sipped her wine then said, "Giving up everything for a baby and not having help must have been hard."

My mom's death replayed in my mind. I had had such a round belly and waddled around making all the decisions about her burial, and every minute of the way on my feet I'd wished things had been different.

"I gave birth alone. It was hard. I wanted my mom with me, but she couldn't be there."

"Well you have us now," Sarah said.

My shoulders relaxed. Michael gave me a smile and said, "And Mom, Georgie was a financial analyst. I'm hoping she can help me manage my portfolio."

"That would be nice." My lips curled at the idea other people might carry some of the load.

We all ate our steak as my mouth had watered for more until my belly filled up.

As we winded down with the food, Tom asked, "Can we ask you both a personal question?"

For the past moment, I'd forgotten all my fears. It had been a while since someone had listened to my issues and not the other way around. I nodded and asked, "What's that?"

Tom placed his napkin on the table like he was done eating and asked, "Why didn't you find Michael sooner? Did you not watch baseball?"

Now that was fair. I wish I had gone to find him. Life would have been easier if I'd known him as those late nights alone had taken a toll on me. "I haven't gone to a game in years. I only went to a game now, because Jeremy wanted to go, and my sister Indigo scored us good tickets. I thought it would be good bonding time. I had no idea until I stared at the jumbotron and saw his stubble and jawline again that my life would change that day."

I sipped my wine and I thought we were done, but then Michael snapped his fingers and said, "Speaking of, the DNA test arrived."

I swallowed to not embarrass myself and choke, but I turned toward him and said, "You didn't say anything."

He shrugged and said, "We knew instantly." Then he told his parents, "There is no denying Jeremy is my boy, Georgie. It was for the lawyers."

I stared into my glass and wished I could just disappear right now. I was so close to turning into my mother as I said, "I never tried to find Michael. When I left the Bahamas, my head was such a mess as my dad was dying, and I just wasn't thinking straight. Six weeks after leaving him, I'd buried my dad, found out I was pregnant and then my mom took ill…"

Sarah tapped her husband's shoulder and said, "Michael should have been better at finding you."

"That year was the hardest of my life except for having my son." I'd probably misjudged his mother who was nothing but kind. I should be better. Help was a good thing. Michael took my hand in his and said, "I… you're right, Mom. I spent countless nights wishing thing were different rather than tracking down the woman I love. I won't make that mistake ever again."

Love. Right. He'd snuck into my heart, despite how I thought it was firmly insulated from ever opening. This was what we had, and Jeremy was a product of a good union; one where I refused to perish away and said, "You can't change the past, Michael."

Jeremy swallowed his last bite and curled his lips higher. "We're a family now."

The sun started to set but Michael laughed as he said, "True son. And I'm glad we're together."

Right. We were married. This wasn't about dying but about living. Love wouldn't destroy me. I refused to let it.

Chapter 14

_____

Michael

My body surged from activities I'd only imagined for years. Now that Georgie was in my life, I'd yet to have my fill.

Maybe I never would and that was okay. We were married so she was mine, forever now.

I couldn't imagine loving another woman and didn't want to ever think about it. She'd been it for me since we'd met.

As I rolled over in my duvet cover, the spot beside me was empty, again. *She must wake up early these days.* I opened my eyes and the flood of daylight in the room made me want to reach for a pillow and hide for another moment.

But I heard her sweet humming in the en suite bathroom.

I stood and ignored my morning hard-on, though it was harder when I let myself in and realized she was naked and in my shower.

I'd join her if she wanted. I brushed my teeth and waited for an invitation, but she continued to sing to herself.

I got the hint she wanted a few minutes alone, so I headed to the closet for my jeans and t-shirt.

A few minutes she came out, in black jeans and a black t-shirt. She also had her small bathroom bag all packed as she said, "This weekend went so fast."

My heart raced faster and I stood taller and said, "I'll be back in Tulsa in four days for three days at home."

She grabbed her small bag and checked her makeup was in it as she said, "We'll be in Pittsburgh. Our flight leaves early this afternoon."

I wrapped my arms around her waist and wished she was staying. "I was hoping now that we're married, I could see you the days I'm in town."

She twirled in my arms and hugged my shoulders when she said, "We discussed this. Let's not change the plan now."

"We didn't set up a plan."

"I thought we did."

"I'm good at remembering concrete terms." Jeremy. Right, but my son was happy here and my house was double the size of hers. I ignored the zip in my vein and said, "Kids adapt well. You don't have to stay in Pittsburgh."

She let me go and finished arranging her bag as she said, "Michael…I need to go home and let my mind rest. We agreed we wouldn't move until November."

"Because of school or because you want time apart?"

"A lot's happened and I want to talk to my sisters in person, figure out what I want to do for school in the spring. But remember you promised to move in with us come November till April, until you know where we're going to live."

"November is months away." At least she still planned on living with me in the end. I ignored the thought of how I should be wary of giving this woman my heart as she turned around and stared at me so casually. I asked, "And you're okay living apart for the next two months?"

She nodded and that made me pause. I'd hoped once we'd discussed feelings, life would change. But she was calm and cool, as she said, "I want to provide stability for Jeremy. He's the most important person in both our lives, right?"

She tugged her collar checking it was fine. I widened my stance. "I was hoping this weekend would convince you to stay in Oklahoma for the rest of the season, so I can see you both more often."

"I can't…decide right now." I reached for her bag, so she couldn't carry it and she adjusted her shirt. "The first weekend in October has a planning day for the teachers that Friday. What are you doing then?"

Probably the playoffs though the schedule wasn't out yet. "I don't know fully yet where I'll be, but I'll keep you posted."

She opened the door of the bedroom to leave as she asked, "I thought baseball schedules were organized and tickets sold before players ever hit the dirt?"

"Regular season, yes." I walked beside her. "October is for the playoffs or we're benched. We're good right now and should be playing but anything might happen this month. So we need to be prepared."

"Jeremy pack your bag," she called out to the next room, and then turned to me as she glided onto the stairs. "I'm glad we're not rushing because we got married. Honestly…"

We made it to the bottom, but my skin had goosebumps now. "Yeah?"

She came closer to me and said, "Look, I love you. I just need to figure out how we fit."

Together. I kissed her cheek and hugged her as I said, "That's the easy part, Georgie."

She curled into my arms, and for a moment I was warm, and everything was good. As the kiss ended, she slipped out of my arms and said, "Maybe you see your life all planned out perfectly, because you're on the road a lot. I need to figure out our end though. For now, Jeremy and I need to eat breakfast and head to the airport."

She headed into the kitchen and my stomach tightened like I'd swallowed a stone. I'd not eat a bite, but I followed her inside and said, "I can't come in for a week."

She took pans out like she'd make something. I was going to say something once my skin stopped growing goosebumps, but then my phone rang.

She took out the mixer and waffle maker and said, "Get it. It's okay."

I answered Phil, "The Yankees want you bad, Michael. They offered everything you want but there is a time clock running on this offer."

Ten years, thirty million a year. The deal of a

lifetime. I blocked out when she turned the mixer on as I asked, "How long do I have?"

"Seventy-two hours," Phil said.

Georgie had complained about New York. Phil had heard her. I stared at her as she made dough and turned on the waffle maker as I asked, "Can you tell them I need to talk to my family, and that I'll need a week?"

Phil hadn't mentioned Georgie directly or her complaints yesterday as he said, "I'm sure that's fine. It's known you're married so it shouldn't be a problem to sell newlyweds to get you more time."

Code for *speak to Georgie*. I swallowed and said, "Thanks, Phil."

I hung up and stared at her. She finished pouring the batter into the machine and then straightened as she asked, "What's going on?"

I widened my stance. This was it. No more waiting. I met her gaze and said, "New York offered thirty million for ten years."

Her chin fell as she asked, "New York?"

This wasn't her ideal. I got that. I came closer and held my palms out as I said, "I read an article last night that only one third of the players actually live in Manhattan, and it's usually the single ones. There are homes farther out, with space not that far and we can house hunt, together."

Her eyes misted and she turned to watch the steam out of the waffle maker as she said, "So you want New York."

I patted her back. Before we married, we'd discussed Pittsburgh and how open I was as long as I got the money. Money proved I was one of the best players in the league and I needed that evidence in my paycheck. I'd wished the Sooners got that, but money meant I was valued. I kept my voice low as I said, "I want the money to secure our future, ensure Jeremy has the best school money can buy, a car when he's old enough…"

She stopped trembling and opened the machine to take out the first waffle and add more batter as she said, "Let me think about it."

"Think fast. The offer has a time limit," I said and made the coffee.

We heard Jeremy moving around upstairs as we set the plates, juice, and coffee on the table, and she finished the last waffle. She didn't look at me as she said, "I am okay with most of the country. I always get overwhelmed in New York, and I want to research schools, make a spreadsheet."

Research wasn't a full no, and she'd mentioned her process in the past. I hoped she'd agree to the changes so we could be together more, as I asked, "Yeah?"

Her face had a bit of a blush when she said, "I need to figure out what's best for Jeremy. That will always be my priority."

The best education was important. I playfully pressed our shoulders together and said, "I understand. Maybe we can figure out a way for schools to transition and get a private tutor/nanny to ensure a seamless transition?"

Her face went white as she asked, "You'd subject our son to losing an entire class of his peers and being all by himself, with a tutor, for ten years?"

That was the wrong answer. I needed to figure out how to be a better parent. "I'm just spit balling suggestions on how we can make it work."

She nodded like she accepted my answer and then pressed her hand on my back. "Let's have breakfast and you can drive us to the airport."

Jeremy was still upstairs, but it sounded like he was on the stairs now. I wrapped my arms around her and said, "Okay, Georgie. Kiss me first."

"Kisses don't make everything better," she said but her face came up to meet mine.

Her warm breath on my skin sent my body into overdrive. She wrapped her arms around my neck, and I lowered my lashes, "No, but they can open up softer communication, so we don't argue."

And then I kissed her. This was perfect. She was my everything. She let out a small sigh as I let her go and she patted my shoulder alerting me that Jeremy was behind me. "We'll talk. I promise."

I waved at my son to join us at the table and said, "Good because I want the money."

I needed the validation. Her lips pressed together but she brought the waffles and sat down with us. We didn't talk about it as we ate.

We didn't need to, I guess. I was owed in cash and the Sooners hadn't put the money up to prove they'd wanted me. So, we were going.

Jeremy and Georgie just needed time, and I could give them 72 hours or more if Phil pulled that off. And then I was signing on the dotted line.

Chapter 15

Georgie

Michael's house here was amazing. We'd have room to breathe.

Texas had sounded amazing because his family would join us, and we'd have space. But New York?

The streets were always crammed with people. The hotel rooms were tiny. Everything was jam-packed.

Even Central Park had no corners to hide in. Strangers had sat next to me when I'd tried to rest on a park bench. I'd left my job interview on Wall Street with a huge headache that no meditation technique quite worked out of my system.

I'd sworn to never ever go back and now Michael expected me to move to a place I might hate.

How in the world would I be a good parent if I was stressed out all the time?

No amount of money was worth my health.

I needed to live for my son.

Michael parked near the entrance of the airport and took our bags out. "Jeremy, I'll see you in a week in Pittsburgh."

Jeremy hugged him and said, "That will be good, Michael."

And that was another thing. My son wasn't comfortable calling his own father "Dad". That was probably a sign I pushed for some impossible dream, and I needed to not push.

My heart raced as Michael handed me my bag and said, "We might need to make some calls about New York's offer."

"New York?" Jeremy switched his bag to his other arm and stared at us.

Michael knelt down and told our son, "Yeah, they came back with the perfect contract."

Jeremy didn't even blink. "Do I get a brand-new car when I'm old enough then?"

Michael laughed, nodded, and hugged him as he stood. "Whatever one you want."

Jeremy held out his thumb and said, "I'm good then."

I blinked. My skin prickled like pins and needles stabbed at me. This wasn't that easy.

"That's it? You want a car?"

Jeremy stared at me like I was speaking a foreign language and then asked, "Was there something else you wanted, Mom?"

Yesterday, he'd been upset about his friends and leaving school. I didn't want to rehash that. My heart was heavy, and I hugged my waist as the word "no" screamed in my mind. I then said, "I...I want to talk to a realtor about a home with bedrooms, and a small lawn, and a nice kitchen as I like to cook."

The airport was full of people milling past without giving us a glance.

My entire body trembled. I glanced around and hoped no one noticed me. Then Michael came with his arms open to hug and kiss me as he said, "We can get you a palace and have the kitchen done before we move in, if you agree."

How was he okay at a time like this? I was a walking disaster. My heart pounded as I massaged my forehead and said, "No, not yet. I need time."

He squeezed my hand and asked, "Time to what? We can do this together."

My eyebrows raised. This was crazy.

"Don't push."

He came to kiss me, but his phone rang. He held my hand and stared at Jeremy as he said, "Phil's calling. Just give me ten seconds to say goodbye."

Michael stepped back to talk.

I tried to breathe but my chest didn't quite fill with air. Jeremy tugged on my sleeve. "Mom, what's wrong?"

"Everything's fine, Jeremy," I told him but that wasn't the truth.

My skin had goosebumps and adrenaline rushed through me. If I lived in New York, my stomach would be twisted and I'd be on edge like this every moment of every day, for ten years.

Jeremy said, "If you hate New York, tell Michael."

Again, it wasn't dad or father or papa. Jeremy'd said "Michael". That was good, right? If I said no, my son couldn't be that mad at me. I was irrational but moving would be bad. I took a breath and took a small comfort they hadn't developed a proper bond, and that probably made me a bad mom.

I should say something. Michael came back, phone in his pocket, and took my hands as he said,

"Phil said no extension. I need to give an answer in seventy-two hours."

My stomach muscles tightened, and I practically trembled, but I pretended I was fine and went to my tiptoes to kiss him goodbye as I said, "Call me after your game tonight."

"You'll be up?" He asked and held me.

"Yeah." This wasn't as easy as I thought. I shouldn't be this crazy. I needed to find my voice, but I said fast, "I'll have a chance to think."

"That's fair. I'll miss you both," he said, and then his lips met mine.

For this one moment, the rest of the world disappeared. I was the same girl who'd met him in the Bahamas and splashed water in the pool at him until he kissed me.

The memory roared back and made me forget where I was, until the kiss ended.

And the people on their phones, the families talking, the wheels that were screeching all roared in my ears.

I held my lips together and waved goodbye.

Then, Jeremy took my hand and we walked over to check-in together.

Michael watched us as we headed inside, and I held my head up.

I had to admit flying first class had less lines, less stress, and even security was easier on us.

I hardly noticed take off, flying, or landing.

My son was safe. We were comfortable and soon we were back in familiar gray skies. We headed out and, at the curb, was my brown haired, brown-eyed sister who didn't care that her curls were too long to frame her face as she wore bright turquoise glasses and hugged me. We tossed our bags in her trunk and we hopped in her car.

A minute later, we drove onto the familiar needed-new-tar-on-the-road-but-it-was-never-in-the-city-budget bumpy highway. It tossed my backside on the drive and reminded me I was home.

She asked, "Georgie, Jeremy, what's going on?"

I ignored how my entire body was tense and pivoted toward my sister and said, "Indigo, it's good to see you."

She took one glance at me and said, "So we'll stop and get a bottle of wine while you talk to me."

Jeremy called out from the back, "Mom's upset that Michael needs to move to New York."

"I have wine at home," I said.

She took the backroad off the highway toward my house, and my skin crawled as she said, "I thought you were in love and happy with this baseball player."

I lowered my voice so Jeremy didn't hear me as I said, "I can't be Mom."

"You aren't," Indigo said like it wasn't a big deal and drove into my garage as she said, "Unlike Mom, you show up for everything in Jeremy's life. I'd say you're more like Dad and his big heart."

That would be nice, but I didn't see myself taking in every troubled kid in the world. She turned off her car and helped us with our bags. "I don't see that. He was in charge and more commanding than I'd ever be. Even if I could be more like him, I don't know if that's enough to protect me."

"From what?"

"From disappearing because I'm married."

Jeremy shook his head like he didn't get it, but Indigo held the bags as I opened the door.

"Don't sell yourself short," Indigo said. "You'd have found a way to shine on your own because you're special. Though, you marrying a baseball player is pretty awesome."

"Why?"

"It gets me cool points in my office."

Jeremy tossed his shoes and said, "I'm going to my room, Mom."

He took off without waiting for an answer.

But right now, I wasn't upset. Indigo walked me

to my kitchen and poured us glasses of wine. She handed it to me, and I asked her, "Why is my marrying Michael awesome besides your cool points? You don't care about what people think about you."

"True." Indigo walked with me into the living room where we'd spent countless hours sitting on my couch talking as she said, "I've done nothing but read up on your husband. He's seriously hot. My bosses want me to use the new family connection to get him on cereal boxes."

Oh. This was about impressing her impossible boss at the advertising company that she hated. I shrugged and said, "Michael will be here in a week, you can ask him yourself."

"I don't have a lot of time tonight to stay and dig everything out slowly like I normally would." She sipped her wine and stared at me. I did the same as I wasn't sure what to say anymore. Then she said, "For a bride, you don't seem happy, Sis."

What could I do? Lie to my sister? I massaged the side of my face and hoped I hadn't winced. Then I stared at my white colored wall and said, "I…I don't want to leave my house and move to New York."

She shrugged like it wasn't a big deal. "Tell him that."

I sipped and nodded my head as she was right. It took a while to get there but finally I flipped to face her and said, "I need to not be wishy-washy."

She finished her glass, stood, and said, "Well, you're safe and I have to go."

Go? Indigo hadn't said anything when I'd texted. I walked her to the door and asked, "Where?"

She hugged me and took her keys out as she said, "I...I'm going with my boss to Vegas."

Normally, she complained all the time about her boss, but today she hadn't complained once. I narrowed my gaze and asked, "This is fast. Are you eloping?"

Her face went white like I'd shocked her, and she shook her head as she said, "Don't be crazy. It's work, though I did book the Venetian because your wedding pictures made me slightly envious."

My wedding. I'd been so lust-filled with love blooming in my eyes I hadn't thought straight. Indigo checked her hair in the side mirror and I said, "I wanted to spend more time there."

"Have fun," I called out.

She waved and unlocked her car as she said, "It's work, but I'll check a few places out."

I watched a movie, showered, checked on Jeremy, who was doing his homework, made us dinner, got ready for bed, and finished my bottle of wine without anyone interrupting the day.

It was like today was normal again.

As I turned off the lights in my house to go to bed, my phone finally rang. I saw Jeremy's light was out and headed to my room where I answered. "Michael, your game went late."

That sounded awful. My stomach flipped as that was no way to greet him. My palms sweated like I'd run a mile.

"I'm three hours behind you today." He said it like that didn't mean it was after midnight.

I ignored how my heart raced. This wasn't calm or good. I closed my eyes as I said, "Right. Sorry."

What if I never figure out how to be calm? I cringed against the wall.

Michael asked, "Are you okay?"

I opened my eyes and ignored how my body trembled for real as I said, "Yes. I mean no."

He asked me, "What's going on?"

Time to speak my mind. I'm not my mother. I lifted my chin, not that he could see me. But I stilled and said fast, "I don't want to go to New York."

"Georgie, I told you I wanted the money. I need the contracts to prove I'm the best in baseball."

There it was. The line. If I crossed it, I might just turn into my mother, the silent woman who went to the other room. I closed my eyes to shut out the world. I'd never meet his needs and he couldn't meet mine. I shook but I said, "Then go without us. I can't live there."

Michael said, "You're being unreasonable."

My eyes opened. I was safe in my living room with my white walls. His words didn't push me or make me tremble. I could breathe. This was the right choice.

"So are you. If you loved me, you'd not ask this of me."

He said, "That's being crazy. I can get whatever your heart desires if I take this job."

Money. That was his only goal. Not mine, not Jeremy. I picked up my wine glass and brought it to my sink. Then I said, "Then take it, but I'm not going anywhere near you."

"What are you saying?"

I needed a broom and to stop shaking. I swallowed and said, "We shouldn't have gone crazy and gotten married. It was a mistake."

He asked in a higher pitched tone, "You're leaving me because I want New York?"

"Yes," I said and froze. I'd never be calm there. Once I stopped seeing Michael, then I'd be safe and not be pushed.

"You're being unreasonable."

"Goodbye Michael. We're not going to New York," I said and hung up to get my broom.

Maybe I was wrong about marrying Michael and thinking we had a shot. I was never going to quietly transform into someone who doesn't speak out about her life or her son. If I moved with him, it would start. We were all better off this way.

Chapter 16

Michael

Never make phone calls in the car. I'd almost crashed a mile after I'd hung up the phone on my way back to the hotel. Luckily, I came to and slammed on the breaks.

Georgie's pretty smile replayed in my mind from the day we met at the pool. And now our wedding in Vegas when she walked under the green archways toward me on that gondola.

Sleep hadn't washed those pictures from my mind. Neither had driving to work the next day.

My blood ran cold as I headed to the parking lot for players.

We're not going to New York. No discussion? Just

no. I turned off my engine but stared at the palm trees of LA and tried to move. But I couldn't. My memories of Georgie in the stands that day replayed. There she'd been, with my son.

I never saw it coming that she'd just say no and was willing to get divorced.

I'd spent my entire adult life working to be the best. Contracts showed how much teams valued the players and I wanted to be one of the highest in the league, because it meant for sure I was the best.

I'd been trained since I was smaller than Jeremy for this and I was inches from achieving everything I'd worked for.

What the fuck had happened? How did I fix this?

I loved Georgie. I'd waited for seven years to find her again. But did that mean I had to give up everything I'd ever worked for?

Now I needed to play. I needed to scream. I should have ignored her that day, but she'd been the angel I'd searched for, for years.

But that had been a lie. An angel wouldn't make me choose like this.

Finally, I made it out of the car and dragged my ass into the game.

Somehow, I needed to get rid of this cold sweat that made my spine tingle and win.

Thirty million for ten years had always been the first dream.

I'd spent my entire life working toward being the best.

I went to my locker to grab my uniform.

Rodriguez came beside me and stared at his old beat up Swatch watch that he wore at every game instead of any of the fancy ones everyone had bought him. "About fucking time, Irons."

"I need a shower," I mumbled and stripped off my t-shirt that still had a small trace of Georgie's hugs on it.

I'd have to burn it if the smell didn't dissipate. I tossed my sneakers in the locker and Rodriguez said, "Go clear your head, Pinstripes."

Maybe moving to New York and working with teammates I didn't consider friends might be better. Less opinions I didn't want to hear. I unbuttoned my pants and said, "Don't be hating. Maybe if you up your stats, you'd have a shot at the stripes too."

Rodriguez stomped off. I wrapped a towel around my waist to not flaunt my junk in front of everyone when my phone rang. I sat in front of my locker and for a second wished it was Georgie, to tell me she'd been wrong.

But once again my insides froze as I read the screen. I squeezed the phone in my palm and told myself to get over this and then answered, "Phil, what's going on?"

My agent asked, "Do you have a minute? I want to talk about your voicemail."

More players arrived but I didn't care as I slouched in my corner and said, "Yeah. I told you… let's sign."

"Hold off till tomorrow," Phil said.

"Why?" I asked.

He would make the best commission of his career if I did this. Money mattered.

I needed to be the best. Though, my son and I when we tossed the ball played in my mind. I'd already missed years of him, and my skin grew hotter with regret.

I couldn't miss more of his life.

Phil said, "I'm getting signals I'll have another offer by the morning and it's still within the seventy-two-hour window."

"Yeah?" I asked and wondered for a second if it would matter.

I hadn't told anyone, but I loved working with the Sooners and Georgie'd liked my house. If I had the money and Georgie back, then my life would be exactly as I hoped.

Or was tomorrow too late?

Phil said, "It might be more, might be nothing, but let's see it first."

I lowered my voice. "Whatever you think is best. I'm loyal to the paycheck you get me for my skills."

"How's Georgie?" Phil asked.

Good question. I closed my eyes and remembered how her kiss still tingled on my lips. "She won't go to New York and wants a divorce if I pick there."

Phil said, "I'm sorry. You should talk to Gary."

"Who's Gary?" I asked as it wasn't a name I recognized.

"A lawyer friend who specializes in helping pro-sports players with their divorces."

That was a knife on an open wound. I cringed and saw the pitcher returning to the locker next to me as I said, "I don't want to think about that right now."

"It's fine," Phil said. "Just have a good game. Your offers might depend on it."

No pressure, right? Maybe a second offer was on the table if I did. I jumped up, still holding my phone when the pitcher, now in his gray pants, stared at me and pointed to the door. "You still naked? We have fucking warm ups and then a game to get to already."

My mind raced. I was crazy.

I grabbed my soap and said, "Shut the fuck up, Rodriguez. Warm your arm up and stop getting in my shit. I'll be right out."

"You'll be fun to talk to out there tonight," he said as I started to walk away.

I slowed down. Georgie had nothing to do with the game. Teams live and die by working together. I couldn't face him, but I said, "I…I need to clear my head and relax. I promise to get my head in the game out there."

"See you out there then," he called out as I headed into the shower.

The water and steam usually did the trick when it was too many drinks the night before. Clean-faced was almost my standard, and from what I knew of New York, a requirement of theirs I'd clearly meet.

Today, my skin was raw. As I finished and grabbed my uniform to dress, I saw my phone ring again. I tugged on my gray away game clothes and answered, "Dad. What's going on?"

Dad sounded like he had when I was a boy, "Your pregame interview wasn't your usual. Is something going with you, son?"

Maybe he had an answer. I sucked in my breath. Normally I wouldn't ask, but Dad had managed to hang onto my mom for more than thirty years now.

So I kept my voice low so no one could hear when I said, "I got the offer from New York."

"And Georgie doesn't want to go," he surmised.

I rubbed my neck as the coach was calling us out for some sort of team huddle, but I held back and said, "Yeah."

"She was clear about that the other day. What's the second-best offer?"

Just give up on the money? That was his answer. I ignored how my gut was all twisted as I said, "Phil says wait till tomorrow."

"Look, we worked hard for you to be the best. Georgie seems like a good woman, but you need focus."

If Phil had a better offer tomorrow, maybe there was a shot at keeping Georgie, if she ever talked to me again.

Or maybe I gave up millions. My fingers shook slightly as I said, "She and I might have been a fantasy."

"And my grandson? You'll need a good lawyer if she doesn't bend."

My boy mattered, just as much as his mom. I heard the coach in the distance calling out names. He'd get to me in a second, and I had a rush of adrenaline as I said, "I don't have all the answers yet. That's why I'm in a bad mood."

"Shake it off. You have the game of your life and if you want anything other than New York, win big."

I coughed back the rebellion that comment normally caused in me but also drove me to show him he was wrong. "No pressure at all huh, Dad?"

Dear old dad was the same as he said, "That's your mother's job to coddle you. Get your head in the game."

"I have to go," I said, and at least I could flex my muscles.

Dad was hard on me, but he was right. I needed to show up and play ball now, not imagine some fantasy life with a woman who clearly didn't care about me.

I made it to the huddle and the coach didn't call me out.

Then we all went out as the national anthem was being played. I was silent and let the moment sink in.

I was here to play. Baseball had always been the one girlfriend I could depend on. Hit, run, catch. I had this in me.

As I made it back to the dugout, before we were

called out to play my outfielder friend walked over to me and I said, "Rodgers."

He glanced at me and asked, "Where's your phone?"

"Huh?" I asked.

He stared at me like I'd committed a murder in front of him as he said, "At this point in the game you always pull out your phone. You said it was your lucky charm."

Traditions. Right. Georgie's picture in that bikini of hers had been a dream. And part of my game. I took out my phone like if I didn't look at her, I'd lose and said, "Right. Thanks."

His face had color now and he nodded at me. "We need to win, not just for your pinstripes."

There she was.

Younger, pretty, and staring at me like she actually found me the most interesting person in the world.

Done, I put it away and ignored how my body grew warm like she was part of the package of living happily forever. But I put it away and asked about the Yankees as I said, "How does everyone know about that? I haven't signed yet."

"It's been the buzz in the office for hours," he said, like it was obvious.

That didn't matter. The crowd jeered as we were

not the home team, but I jogged out with my friend. "Either way I'm here and I'm here to win."

A few minutes later, the first ball was tossed and almost rammed right into my face, but I caught it. And instincts took over.

Every game was war, and I focused all my attention on it.

The few hours flew fast and it was nighttime as the game ended.

I shook hands with the other team and headed into the locker room.

Rodriguez, after being relieved in the eighth inning, shook the champagne, and let the liquid shower us as we headed inside. I gave Rodgers a high five.

A few minutes later, I was clean and in my jeans with my uniform tossed for Aaron to collect for us.

I avoided the press and headed to my rental car.

My hotel bed was all I had to sleep on, but it wasn't the worst bed I'd ever had.

As I raced away from the stadium, my phone rang. I reached for it and hoped it was Georgie.

But it was a number I didn't recognize. I answered and the stranger said, "Great game tonight."

The man sounded older, but I kept that to myself and said, "Thanks. Who's this?"

"Gary Narmeli, the attorney that Phil said would call."

My skin vibrated and my stomach turned into a knot. My agent must have set this up, but my throat froze. I turned into the hotel parking lot and switched my car off. "Right."

"Look, you're free to hire whoever. Phil and I have worked together for his players for over ten years now."

I headed into the lobby and saw no teammates at the bar. Good. I continued to my room. "I trust Phil's recommendations."

"So what's going on?"

Was that code for talk about Georgie? I pressed the button for the elevator and said, "Nothing I'm ready to talk about yet."

"You sure?"

"I'll call you when I'm ready," I said and hung up as I stepped into the elevator.

If I went this route, I gave up on Georgie.

Maybe tomorrow I'd be ready to talk about how my life had changed and what I'd do next. No one needed to lead me anywhere.

As I got off on my floor, Rodriguez was on my caller ID. Had I left something in the locker room? I answered and he said, "Sorry I doubted you earlier Irons. You were good today."

There he was, the heart of the team. Every team needed one like Rodriguez.

I said, "I wish I could stay with the Sooners, but I need to follow my dreams."

"We hoped you'd stay, but Rodgers is planning a goodbye bash."

"I'll be there," I said and opened my empty hotel room.

Alone.

I was here for two more days. My shoulders slumped and he said, "Take care of yourself. We need your head in every game till the end."

"Count on me," I said and hung up the phone.

Tonight, I'd dream about a life where I actually had the money and Georgie and didn't have to choose. But that was just for dreams.

Tomorrow, I would take the money and prove to myself I was the best there was. It was everything I'd worked for years to achieve and the smart choice. All I needed to do was sign on the dotted line.

Chapter 17

Georgie

Michael was perfect on my television.

I hadn't intended to watch the game.

After I'd showered and let the water rush against my face, I'd turned the small TV on in my bedroom and just stared at him.

My arms ached to hold him. He caught two balls in five minutes and both times he was on screen for a moment.

My heart raced in those seconds. My lips ached to kiss him and beg him to forgive me.

I'd never be happy without him in my life. Calmness was an illusion to hide my desire.

After the inning ended, I called Indigo who told me to call Olivia.

I sucked on my bottom lip as I dialed and hoped she'd help.

If I didn't fix my life, I'd be forever…stuck. This wasn't right.

Love meant taking chances, and I'd not done that.

My mother had been braver than I gave her credit for when she'd been alive. She'd been abused, but had come out of her shell when my dad was around. Love had made her stronger. I don't know how the water slapping my face had made me see that. All of my cousins had come from harder backgrounds, and they'd found refuge with us.

My mom cooked like every one of them belonged in our house.

I'd forgotten her open heart for every Steel child, until tonight.

Jeremy deserved to see love was possible for him too and that his father was good.

So, while my son slept and the game still played, I called my second sister as I tugged my jeans on. When she finally answered, I said, "Olivia, I need help."

"What's going on?" she asked.

I finished getting dressed and turned on my laptop. "Can you come over and watch Jeremy tonight and tomorrow?"

"Why?"

I turned on the lights and went to my bag in the closet to get my laptop as I said, "I need to go to LA."

"Why?" She asked and I deflated in movement and closed my eyes.

I was stupid, in love, and had tossed out the best man I'd ever met, because I was afraid. I squared my shoulders and spoke fast as I grabbed my wallet and said, "Michael is there."

"I thought he was coming to Pittsburgh in a week?"

I clicked on the midnight flight as I said, "I told him I wanted a divorce and hung up on him."

"What? Why?"

She was seriously sounding like an annoying parrot. I hope I didn't ask this many questions. "Because I feared I'd turn into Mom if I loved him too much."

"Aww, well that's silly." Olivia said like she was teaching her fifth-grade class again and then added for measure like this was all math, "You loved him before anything happened to Dad."

I dug out my card but didn't type anything in as I asked, "Can you come and help me, now?"

Olivia said, "Pack your bags. Take a week on the road for your honeymoon. Jeremy and I can go to school together."

"Thank you," I said as I typed in my information.

This wasn't first class, but the midnight flight landed me in Los Angeles at 5:00 am.

"Are you looking things up?"

"You know me well."

It was better to talk in person, hopefully. I didn't want to make another mistake and face-to-face was where I was most alive.

Hopefully, I could tell him he completed my life. I'd been wrong to hang up. The screen finally read "confirmed".

Yes. Olivia then said, "Oh, Indigo's on the line. Hold on." Guess I had no choice. I dug my small traveling bag out again as Olivia clicked back in and said, "All three of us are together now."

Indigo asked, "So Olivia's babysitting?"

"Yes, but you'll help?" I asked as I grabbed my underwear and bras. Maybe I'd be right home and he'd tell me to fuck off. I probably deserved that, but if he didn't, then I wanted cute underwear.

Unfortunately, I didn't own many.

"This morning, but I'm off to Vegas tomorrow." Indigo said, "Ridley and Nicole are both in to help though. Phoenix and his fiancée are coming to town and they want to take Jeremy to a concert."

"That's fine."

"I confirmed with them to keep him overnight on Friday, so Olivia could have some time for herself. "Look, I'll text you the hotel he's staying at now. Did you get your plane ticket?"

Indigo was always the genius in finding out information for me. She'd found me tickets, found out where Michael's team was staying in LA. I needed to buy her a huge birthday present but for now I held a hand to my heart and said, "It leaves in three hours. Olivia needs to get here fast so I can make my flight."

I grabbed clothes without paying much attention to what and tossed it in the bag as Indigo said, "You act like Pittsburgh airport might be a problem when you're flying to LA. Now when you land, that is a monolithic place."

"Right. Okay. Good to know." I swallowed and grabbed my stuff from the bathroom. "I'll be fine."

"Rent the car before you hit the road," Olivia said.

Hurry up already and get here. Normally I'd have spent time researching the best price, but I quickly realized renting was cheaper than a ride share. So I picked the cheapest option, but today I was off center. I sighed into my phone and opened my laptop again. I used an app and found a car. "This is taking forever."

"You'll thank me," Olivia said and I heard her car in the driveway.

I wanted to jump and scream but my son was sleeping. "I do thank you."

The garage door opened. I hung up with them both, grabbed my bags, and threw open the door to my sister who was opening her trunk for me.

Then I ran down the stairs, tossed my bag in the back, and saw that all she'd packed for her trip to Vegas was a small backpack. I hugged her and said, "Goodbye."

She followed me to my garage. "Look, you're my sister, I love you but go fix your mistake."

My skin was awakened, my adrenaline was pumped. I needed to tell him I loved him and wanted him unconditionally. "I'll try. Hopefully, he'll listen."

"If he doesn't, he might need time to heal," Olivia said as she opened the garage door for me. "But you need to try."

He wasn't the one making unreasonable demands. I tossed my stuff in my car and said,

"That's not nice. I was the one that screwed everything up with my fears. I can't believe I was that stupid."

"Go." She waved at me.

And I took off.

Jeremy would understand why I wasn't home with him today. Michael was his father, and he'd want his whole family happy.

Finally, the plane's racing tires squealed until we were in the air.

I kept staring at my switched off phone and the guy next to me snored and sneezed.

This wasn't Michael's first-class seating, but I finally made it to LAX and ran through the huge airport to the car.

The sun was out in the morning sky when I was at the rental agent's desk and nodded to half his questions as he had my driver's license. "Yes, I'll take GPS. That's fine."

He showed me a screen that read "subcompact" and said, "This is all we have right now."

I handed him my credit card. "It works. Thank you."

He handed me my cards and a set of keys. "Good luck, ma'am."

Oh, he had zero idea what I needed that for. My

hair stood on its ends that Michael might tell me to leave.

He had that right. If Michael didn't want to forgive me, I'd find some room to curl up in. But after crying, I'd have to move on.

I'd hung up and been horrible to him and probably didn't deserve him. Being afraid was stupid, and paralyzing, and completely my fault.

The drive was full of cars and at points, not moving, but as I finally pulled into the hotel, the management didn't help. I was ready to show my marriage license to the guy, but then another well-built, all-muscles man came over to me and tapped my shoulder. "Are you the new Mrs. Irons?"

I ignored whatever the guy said behind me. "Yes. Who are you?"

He crossed his arms and stared at my small bag as he said, "Rodriguez. Pitcher. What are you doing here?"

My insides twisted. I was probably too late, but I lifted my chin and said, "I'm looking for my husband."

He pointed to the door and said, "You just missed him."

The air rushed out of my lungs. Seriously. My neck tightened and I asked, "What? Where did he go so early?"

"His agents stationed in LA. He went to his office."

My heart raced wildly. "Would you have Phil's address?"

"Sure." He took out his phone and pointed for me to accept his incoming picture.

A moment later, I had a photo of a business card and I jumped and thanked him.

As I ran back to my tiny car, it took a moment to speed up. I wished it was faster, but I used the navigation system to get me through too much traffic until I finally stood outside a nice glass building and ran inside.

On the second floor, I saw a woman in a black business suit and high heels. "Hi," I said to her. "I'm here to see Phil and Michael Irons."

She pouted at me and said, "You're too late."

My skin zapped like she'd stung me. Maybe the universe was telling me I was too late, but I asked, "What?"

She pointed to the door and shooed me toward it as she said, "They left."

"For where?" I asked and refused to budge.

The women's lips thinned and she glanced at my jeans like she'd never wear anything like them. "Mr. Irons went to the stadium and Phil went to help negotiate his leave."

"No!" I shouted fast. If he was leaving, then I was too late. I practically jumped out of my skin and rushed to the door as I asked, "He's at the stadium?"

"Yes," she said and then went back to filing some papers.

I ran as fast as I could to my car and headed toward the stadium.

Cars were at a standstill on the freeway as I picked up my phone and dialed him. I put it on speaker and tapped my steering wheel as I narrated my life, "Michael, pick up…" But I heard the beep and knew instantly it had gone to voice-mail. I waited and listened to his sexy voice but then I said, "Don't leave LA or your team. We need to talk. I'm coming to the stadium. Wait for me there."

I had no idea if he'd listen to it, but I fought my way to the stadium.

Thankfully, there was no game, so it was empty parking as I parked near the other five cars there.

As I ran inside and no one stopped me, my phone rang. I grabbed it, saw my son's name, and answered.

"Mom, how's LA?"

What in the world could I say? I've not found your father and destroyed your hope for a family? I couldn't do that to him. I stilled and said, "It's warm here."

He asked, "Have you seen Michael, yet?"

"No, I'm having issues," I said and massaged my forehead like that might help me find him.

Jeremy said, "Really? I'll call him right back. We were just talking."

"You were?" I asked.

Jeremy said, "Yeah, he wanted to talk to you, and he had news, but I didn't tell him you were there. I thought you wanted to surprise him."

Ahh. I wanted to scream. I should have asked for help, but I ignored how my skin had pins and needles now as I asked, "Did he say what?"

"No, he wanted to talk to you first. Call me when you find him."

"I love you, Jeremy." No matter what happened next, I'd support my son and his father talking to each other. They were two of the best men in the world and deserved to have each other.

After circling the stadium, I found an office with people. The girl at the desk was dressed in a white t-shirt that was see-through to her black bra.

She waved me in and I asked, "Is Michael Irons here?"

"This way, ma'am." She batted her eyes like she

was sizing me up, then shrugged and guided me through to a small office.

She opened the door and Phil and Michael were sitting together. Phil stood immediately and waved for me to go inside. Michael's blue eyes were as big as those balls thrown in the game. I switched places with his agent and the door closed.

He jumped out of his chair and said, "Georgie?"

Tears came out of my eyes as I said, "I love you. I was so scared yesterday. Please forgive me."

His arms wrapped around me and he said in a low tone, "I love you, too. We need to talk."

My stomach was in knots. I still trembled but I said, "I'm okay with going to New York. I want us to be together."

He lifted my chin and waited till I looked at him. As my tears subsided, he said, "Good, but that's not it."

I swallowed and held him so I wouldn't tremble as I asked, "What?"

He glanced at the door that was closed and then back at me. He pressed his forehead to mine and said, "I have two more offers. One from the Sooners and one from Texas. Which one makes you want to stay with me?"

If he wanted New York, I was there. I hugged

his neck and said, "I don't care. I just want you and us to be together. Forgive me."

He kissed me.

I absolutely didn't deserve a second chance, but if this was the start of one, I'd never, ever, ever screw this up again. Love was about being willing to change and grow together, and with Michael I had everything.

I'd never throw that away again because of fear.

Chapter 18

Michael

My arms still ached to hold the best thing in my life, to ensure she was real and here.

Today had been like a dream come true when she'd walked in the door.

I didn't fucking deserve her or this elation in my blood.

She'd been sweet, and I'd fucked this up. All my life I'd defined myself from this game, and how I was on the field. Georgie had just wanted me.

The only way I changed was if I listened to her and my heart that she possessed.

I kissed her first as I needed to know she was real, and her kiss magnetized me.

I needed her like the wheat fields need sun.

Once I let her breathe, I held her sides and said, "I want you here to listen to the offers."

She didn't let me go past her to get Phil. Instead, she placed her arm on my shoulder and blinked as she asked, "Why are we at the stadium?"

I held my head down and listened to the beat inside my heart as I told her a truth I'd avoided for a while now. "I like my team. They've been good to me in Oklahoma."

Her eyes widened and she asked, "So not New York?"

"Honestly, it's one of the best stadiums I've ever played in and the team is top notch." Right. I'd been so adamant about the dollar proving I'm the best that I'd hurt my family in the process.

If I didn't let go of being the best, every day I'd die and eventually I'd start losing in the game, too. Georgie meant more to me. I honestly had no idea how she'd snuck into my heart these past seven years and how every day I played and prayed she'd somehow find me. If I chose the game over her, then I wasn't honoring my own heart. I said, "The numbers aren't what I wanted, no."

She sucked in her bottom lip and bounced on

her feet until she let it go and spoke, "Then we go to New York."

And let her be miserable? And leave my team for the cold hard cash that, yes, I deserved, but at what price?

My own happiness? Georgie's? I shook my head and said, "I can't force you to go somewhere you don't want. How would you feel about staying with my team?"

She was a sweetheart when she pressed her palm against my cheek and said, "I don't care where we live as long as I'm with you."

I tightened my hand around her waist and said, "We need to make a choice as a family and, in pursuing money only, I almost lost you. I can't lose my son and, if possible, I'd like to be loyal to the team that groomed me."

For a moment, neither of us moved. She closed her eyes, and I held her tight. It was like the warmth of light was in my life again and I never wanted to let her go. However, I kissed her cheek and she went on her tiptoes and kissed me back.

Her lips were firm. I ached for her. But I held back. We were in a side office. I let her go and she took the seat beside where I'd been and playfully elbowed me when she asked, "So what are the offers?"

"Let's get Phil," I said and stood, kissing her forehead as I passed. Then I opened the door and waved for my agent down the hall. "Come in and tell Georgie what's going on."

"Sure," he called out and walked in with a new cup of coffee in his hand. He retook his seat on the other side of the table and said "Hello" to Georgie as he took out his folders. "This morning we are fielding two more competitive offers. One is Houston where they bumped their numbers to twenty-seven million for nine years."

Good. Georgie and my parents had wanted that. And that was a good offer, but I asked, "And the Sooners?"

He opened his paper with the offer and said, "Twenty-eight million for ten years."

I reached for it, but Georgie put her hand on it to stop me and said, "So it's less if we go to Oklahoma?"

I nodded and said, "Yes, but Texas was what you and my parents agreed to."

She let the paper go but asked, "Look, do you want to be loyal to the Sooners? Is that what this is?"

"I want us both to be happy," I said, though she'd been right. My team worked well together and moving across country didn't mean I'd be happier.

She shook her head. "I love your house. A few modifications to make it friendlier to Jeremy, or any other child we might one day have, would be great. But only if you want Oklahoma because you want it."

I took the pen and said, "We can get you a new home entirely if you want that."

She laughed, and I knew she'd finally agreed when she said, "Your house could hold my entire family in one spot and that's saying something. I need space but it's already a lot."

I put my initials on the first page and said, "Oklahoma it is."

She saw me flip the page and said, "New York gets you fame and the exact money you wanted. We'll be happy there because we'll be together."

I initialed the second page and said, "But I get to wear my cowboy hat when I drive to the grocery store."

"Well you could do that in Texas, too," she said.

I stilled. Did she want the other? I'd lose even more. I asked her, "Is that what you want? For my parents to live close by?"

"No," she said, and her face went a little white. She then placed her hand on mine and said, "I want us to be happy and you want to be loyal to your team."

"Exactly," I said and then flipped to the last page with the signature section as I said, "Let's sign, Phil."

"No changing your mind?" Phil asked. "Last chance to change your mind."

I winked at my beautiful, brunette wife and said, "Georgie and I agreed. It's all I need."

"Then let's sign," she said.

I wrote out my first name and Georgie squeezed my hand. "Last chance, Michael. I'm sure there are great schools in New York."

"We'll all be happy here," I said and finished with my name.

"You're sure?" she asked like she was stealing from me.

I handed the paper to Phil and massaged her leg. "Money isn't everything. Making my wife my partner, and our family, is important."

Tears formed in her eyes. "I love you."

"Good. I love you, too," I said and wiped her cheeks.

Phil tapped his fingers on the papers then leaned forward when he said, "I'm going to hold this, but see if I can get you everything you want from Oklahoma. Do you trust me for a few more days?"

Being alone with her was all I wanted. I jumped out of my seat and held out my hand for her. As she joined me, I said, "I trust you. For now, Phil, my wife and I are taking off."

"Have fun," he said and checked the contract. "I'll be in touch soon."

I gave him a thumbs-up and we rushed out. We needed to be alone now.

She stayed beside me as we headed out to the parking lot, but she shook her head when she saw the flight of stairs. She pointed to the stadium loop, and I shook my head. She'd have ten years to learn the tricks of stadium life.

However, I slowed down when we made it to the parking lot. The only extra car was a Toyota Caprice. I pointed to it and asked, "Did you drive in this?"

"It was all they had left." She pushed a button to get her bag out.

I grabbed it for her but then pushed it down as I said, "Doubtful. I'll have it shipped back to the airport today."

I held her door for her and she said, "I saw your team at the hotel."

"Good," I said and joined her. The car turned on

from my light press of a button and we headed out of the parking lot. "We need to catch them at the lunch table to tell them my news."

She asked, "We?"

Jeremy and Georgie were my everything. I headed toward the hotel. "Do you need to get back to the airport?"

"No, my sister Olivia is watching Jeremy for the week."

I drove, pressed the gas a little more and said, "Yeehaw." And then winked at her and said, "So we get a honeymoon now?"

Her face had a cute blush on it. "If you want me to tag along."

I roared the car into the hotel. "Sweetheart, let's tell the team and get back to our room."

She laughed as I grabbed her bag from behind us and carried it into the hotel.

We passed the front desk, and I held her hand the whole way.

On the other end of the long circular rotunda of the lobby was the dining area where my friends sat. I walked toward them with Georgie, and we stood next to the table. "Guys, just came from meeting with the business suits."

"So you're ditching us for New York?" Rodriguez asked.

There it was. I held my hand out to shake his as I said, "Seems y'all fall apart without me here, so I'll stick around some more."

Now that smile of his made me teary a little as he asked, "How long?"

"Ten fucking years, baby," I said and man-hugged Rodgers.

Rodriquez nodded and showed off his dimples when he said, "Then you'd better bring your A-Game to tomorrow's double-header."

"I always play to win," I said and then walked with Georgie out of the restaurant.

Winning included her, always. I'd almost lost her again, and I'd never do that a third time.

Ever.

She was my everything.

Thank you so much for reading. If you're interested in reading the epilogue of Georgie and Michael then you can download it at Rocking Player Bonus Scene.

Having your attention this long is an honor and I hope you find the time to leave your review for this book. Georgie and Michael were dear to my heart as it was about two people with flaws. The next book in the series is Ruthless Financier where Indigo gets a proposition she can't refuse. Marry a billionaire client and get twenty five million dollars. She has impossible dreams that now become possible, but marriage feels real and she's quickly torn. Get Ruthless Financier now.

Or if you're into freebies and reading a dramatic series start with Secret Crush as the Morgans always have a special place in my heart.

Last if you sign up for my newsletter (and get a free book), we can stay in touch.

Ruthless Financier

Indigo

I, Indigo Steel, never believed in romance or love or any of that nonsense. I knew better. I thought my sisters all thought the same thing.

Until Georgie married her baseball player without inviting me to her wedding last week.

Through a strange twist, here I was, in Vegas, staying in the same hotel, to meet a client for work. And I wanted to stroll past the wedding pavilion my sister had sent pictures from of her elopement.

Georgie had always been the emotional one in the family—though the vow to never get married had been her idea.

Another of my sisters, Stephanie, had also decided to forget that discussion, apparently, because she was planning her wedding. At least I was invited to London for that one.

For now, I made it to the gondola rides in the Venetian hotel and watched all the couples kissing.

Gross. Public displays of affections really needed to stay behind closed doors. Yeah, I get it. I was born in the wrong century. But whenever I checked my phone and remembered how much I enjoyed technology, I knew I'd never want to live at another time.

I guess what bothered me about seeing couples on the boats kiss each other was that they were obviously both pretending not to see that we're all flawed and imperfect and there are no soulmates.

Love wasn't real. It was a justification for lust to be socially acceptable to our peers. My phone beeped and I read the message: *I'll meet you in an hour.*

Perfect. My team was great. We'd win this client and head back to Pittsburgh right away. My boss was going to retire, and if I won this client, I'd be the CEO of the entire advertising company.

I'd also be the youngest CEO ever and the first woman. Goals I'd check off my list of accomplishments. I could handle this. I typed a reply as I walked away from the silly water ride. *We can't do*

*anything until the client arrives. If Mr. Ruthless shows
early, I need you back as soon as possible.*

Before any meeting, I always took a short walk.
It helped me clear my head and focus on my pitch,
but I wrote back, *If he shows up early, I'll text you 911.*

I headed into the square that was designed to be
like St. Mark's square in Venice. It was full of
people, just like my experience in the real place, but
half of the tourists here had the glazed eyes that
came from spending too many hours gambling.

As for the square itself, though, all that was
lacking were the Italian guys serenading my Amer-
ican face as I walked down the street.

In six months my sister would be getting
married and I'd head to London for that. Maybe I'd
also return to the real Italy and score another *gelato*
while I checked in on one of my clients there.

I also missed that smell of the water and old city
that Vegas could never recreate.

A deep voice called out behind me, "Hello,
beautiful."

I turned on my high heels and stared at a dark-
haired handsome man with a wicked smile.

Now fuck. He'd be up for the perfect man in
my next fantasy life, when I was safe in bed,
alone. For now, I was happy he was five feet
away and in the doorway of the café, as people

who seemed almost blurry passed in front of him. Wide shoulders, muscles and a dimple made the man hypnotizing. I placed my hand on my hip and said, "Sorry. What did you say?"

I wasn't sorry at all and I had heard him clearly enough. He thought I was pretty. But I wasn't interested.

Then he took a step closer to me and adrenaline rushed through me as he said, "You're perfect, I think."

Walk now, my mind screamed, but goosebumps grew on my body and desire overtook me fast. I ignored the sensation as well as I could and asked, "For what?"

He perused my body and my black-with-green-trim business suit as he said, "For my need of a wife."

I laughed. Now that was the funniest thing I'd ever heard. Me, a wife. Once I caught my breath, I realized those brown eyes of his were almost magnetic. I shook my head. "Wow. Just like that? You don't know anything about me."

He took my hand. "I have an instinct. And you're sexy as hell."

My makeup was to impress my client, not this man who sent a thrill up my arm from a simple touch. "Well, I haven't heard flirting in awhile. If you keep talking like that, I'll sit for a minute."

He walked me into the cafe with him and said, "Then let's get you a drink."

This was all nonsense, but soon real life would barge in. I was here in Vegas to reform a bad boy businessman who'd pay for a corporate makeover. And while this man was attractive, who the fuck knew if he was a psycho or something equally bad? I went with him to his table with the white cloth, near the window to the square, and said, "No drinking for me. I have to meet a client."

His lips curled and showed off his dimples as he asked, "Are you a call girl?"

With my buttons up to my neck? I focused on him and crossed my arm under my chest like I'd bolt out of there. "Seriously? Are you drunk? Is that what's going on? I'm in a business suit."

His knee tapped mine under the table and he winked at me. "Well, honestly, with those thigh-high stockings you're wearing, I figured I'd give it a shot."

My eyes widened as I asked, "How did you know?"

He folded his hands in front of him. "Laser-sharp focus for beautiful women. It's been a problem for me."

Like my client. It's why I was going to suggest to Mr. Ruthless he refrain from being photographed with another woman for the next few years. I shifted my legs to stand up and I shrugged. "I see. Well, I should probably get going. But it was nice to meet you."

He reached out and placed his hand on mine as he said, "Wait. I've been sitting here for over two hours waiting to figure out what kind of woman I need to marry, and you're the only one that struck me as exactly right."

Yet I was not looking to add *Mrs.* anything to my name. Indigo Steel was a great name. Though I often just signed *I. Steel* to everything, which made people not realize I was a woman. Then I knocked them out with my brilliance.

I stood, ready to get going to my meeting, and my shoulder bounced once as I said, "But I'm not looking for a husband. I enjoyed the flirting. But I have to get to work."

I turned to leave, but he followed and asked, "What is it you do?"

This *was* like Italy, with the teasing and flirting. Guess I'd gotten to relive those memories of years ago after all.

"I'm here to pitch an idea for work," I said.

He walked beside me out of the restaurant and

put his hands in his pockets as he said, "Well, if it matters to you, I can pay enough so you don't have to work ever again."

"Why?"

"I need to win."

"I don't gamble."

"It's not about the slots. It's about wresting control of a business empire once and for all."

Sounded like a lot of work—and the type I'm not qualified to do.

I also had no interest in being any man's wife. And the closest thing I had to a maternal instinct was buying my nephew the loudest gifts I could at Christmas, just to annoy my sister.

Besides all that, he clearly wanted sex, and I wasn't into either scenario. He'd star in my dreams only. I generally found that not being involved with anyone was better for me. I shrugged as I kept up my pace. "Good luck. I'm still not a call girl."

He playfully bounced into me and my pulse quickened when he said, "Not as a one-night thing. As my wife."

Impossible. I had no idea why I was suddenly all breathy. As I stared at him, I decided it was his handsome, tall, muscular frame. He turned me on physically, clearly. I said, "I don't even know your name."

I slowed as he said, "Jacob."

Same name as Mr. Ruthless. His real name was Jacob B. Donovan. Most people had no idea that Donovan meant "warrior," but after reading my future client's issues, I'd given him the moniker "ruthless," as that fit his personality.

In the pictures I'd glanced at, Donovan was a handsome man, like this stranger. But there was no way a man fishing for a wife in a hotel lobby was Mr. Ruthless. My client was corporate. And he was in the process of hiring a PR firm—me—to fix his image. The idea was ludicrous, so I let it go as I said, "Common enough first name, I guess."

He asked, "And yours?"

"Indigo," I said. I had no idea why I wanted to talk to this Jacob. I definitely wasn't interested in him. I wasn't into one-night stands, or even dating, if I'm honest.

Sexy men like him put me off-center, and I hate being out of control. The men I'd gone out with ended up boring me to sleep, every time. Lately, I'd started offering suggestions to the men I'd been set up with on how they could brand themselves differently so people might take them seriously, as a way to end the date.

I was good at fixing corporate disasters.

He walked me to the elevator banks that led up

to the conference rooms, not the hotel rooms, as he said, "Unusual."

I pressed the button to go up to my meeting now. "No, just old-fashioned. Which I clearly am."

He leaned against the wall and his gaze smoldered. Damn. I wasn't this weak. Then he asked, "Well, how much would it cost for you to be my bride?"

I swallowed and stared at myself in the shiny, fake gold elevator doors. "You sound serious."

I listened to the machine noises and ignored my body's awareness of Jacob as he said, "I am."

This wasn't real. I fought down the butterflies in my chest that made me slightly off-center with him and said, "I don't want a lifetime with a stranger."

He crossed his arms and looked down at me. I swear he could see through my clothes to my black lacy bra, which I'd only worn to make myself feel good.

"Two years," he said, "with a maximum of five. How much would it cost for you to live with me in my mansion for that long?"

My face heated. This had to be a Vegas bet he was part of. I shouldn't have my panties twisted when I envisioned this man in my bed. I said, "Mansion? Yeah, okay. You're probably dirt poor."

The elevator was almost here. I could tell from

the rumbling that was building in intensity, almost matching my fantasies of Jacob.

"So, indulge me with a number."

I knew I shouldn't indulge him in this, but maybe that was the bet. The truth was, I'd need a fortune to meet all of my responsibilities and make all my dreams happen. If I answered, he'd go away. I stared at him and didn't blink my blue eyes. "Twenty-five million for five years. I figure five million a year."

He snapped his fingers. "Done."

The elevator doors opened and I stepped inside as I said, "Yeah, okay. Look this was fun but I have to go."

He leaned into the elevator for a moment and said, "Indigo, you are exactly what I need, so I'll find you soon to finalize this deal."

The hotel was huge. Who knew how many people milled around the whole strip? I pressed my button and said, "Right. Okay."

My phone hadn't gone off to say Mr. Ruthless had arrived, but it wouldn't hurt to be early. I closed my eyes as I rode up in the elevator.

Maybe my sisters were the hearts and flowers and happily-ever-after types. Or they believed in true love instant spark, like my parents did. But I wasn't ever going to be anything like either of my parents.

I'd learned from my past.

The doors opened and I headed into the conference room where Ajax and my cousin and assistant, Jasmine, waited for me.

My team had set up the displays, printed the proposal and organized the conference room.

They'd even set out glasses of water. All was perfect. Jasmine handed me my hot green tea as she said, "Indigo, there you are."

I nodded at her and put my tea down in front of my chair as I said, "Hi. I was waylaid. Some drunk in a bar asked me to marry him. I said I would for twenty-five million."

Ajax fixed his glasses, though his tie was still crooked, as he said, "This is Vegas, anything is possible. Maybe he was some billionaire like Jacob Donovan."

Ajax was just out of college. I'd train him to handle his own accounts eventually, but he wasn't ready yet. Now, Jasmine was the perfect assistant and had no desire to move up as she wasn't sure she wanted the responsibilities.

I'd never had that luxury. I pointed to Ajax and Jasmine helped him with the tie. I think she liked my new apprentice.

"Yeah, right," I said. "He was probably just some gambler and asking me to name a number for some stupid bet going on somewhere."

This was Vegas, after all.

Jasmine fixed Ajax's tie, so we were all good. As we took our seats, she said, "It would be nice to have twenty-five million dollars."

I flipped through my script to refresh my talking points as I said, "I guess. My inheritance let me buy a condo in Pittsburgh, but I need to work to pay the rest of the bills."

I'd pushed some of that money from my parents' insurance at my sister Georgie for a while, but she didn't need the money now.

Ajax said, "Your new brother-in-law plays professional baseball, though."

Huh? How did he bring up Georgie and Michael? I raised my eyebrow and said, "Yeah? What's the point?"

Jasmine said, "So, it would be fun if you and I could go meet some baseball players. Like, the single kind."

Ajax's face went red as he said, "I meant maybe we can land his team's account. I'd love to work for a baseball team, and get into sports advertising and negotiating celebrity endorsements."

"Ajax, that's not my specialty, but we can see—

when you're ready to take on your own clients, and do more market research." He was clearly young still. I added, "And Jasmine, since we're family, we'll have to talk to Georgie and see if she can set you up with a ball player. Next time you see her, ask her yourself."

My sister and her son were so happy these days. I'd not ask for favors for myself, but Jasmine could.

"You're the best!" she said.

Ajax's lips thinned.

I had zero time for whatever was going on between my assistants. I checked that the proposal was up to date and said, "Now we need to convince Jacob Donovan of that, so he knows our plan is his best shot to save his image, and his company."

I read through my proposal. Mr. Ruthless destroyed companies for breakfast and his name was pretty generally hated, even in the billionaire crowd. He'd exploit weakness whenever it suited him. But then he'd been caught up in a sex scandal. He'd been at a party with a now-known sexual predator who trafficked women. The picture of him and the guy having drinks with scantily clad women around him made his investors flee.

The good thing was that he wasn't actually involved in that case. The party was the first and only time they'd met. The picture had been damaging, but if Ruthless followed my plan, he'd be free of this scandal in no time.

He'd hire me and my team for this.

I was sure of myself. I could fix this disaster. I was good at my job.

Get Ruthless Financier now.

Also by Victoria Pinder

Returning for Valentine's (FREE if you go to my website)

The House of Morgan

Secret Crush

Secret Baby

Secret Bet

Secret Wish

Secret Dad

Secret Heir

Secret Tryst

Secret Date

Secret Romeo

Secret Caress

Secret Match

Secret Bridesmaid

Secret Admirer

Secret Cowboy

Secret Mistress

Secret Cinderella

The House of Morgan Boxed Set 1-3

The House of Morgan Boxed Set 4-6

The House of Morgan Boxed Set 7-9

The House of Morgan Boxed Set 10-12

The House of Morgan Boxed Set 13-15

Princes of Avce

Forbidden Crown

Forbidden Prince

Forbidden Royal

Forbidden Duke

Forbidden Earl

Forbidden Monsieur

Forbidden Marquis

Forbidden Count

Forbidden King

Forbidden Bastard

Forbidden Noble

Forbidden Lord

Princes of Avce 1-3

Princes of Avce 4-6

Princes of Avce 7-9

Steel Series

Rocking Player

Ruthless Financier

Wicked Cowboy

Powerful Prince

Cocky M.D.

Scottish Seducer

Legendary Rock Star

Cinder of Ashes

Playing for Keeps (Fierce Fighter)

Treasured (Look for announcement soon)

The Hawke Fortune

Tempting Gabe

Tempting James

Tempting Conner

Tempting Harry

Tempting Navid

Hawke Series

Brothers in Revenge

Irresistibly Lost

Irresistibly Found

Irresistibly Charming

Irresistibly Tough

Irresistibly Played

Irresistibly Rugged

Irresistibly Strong

Irresistibly Dashing

Irresistibly Boxed Set 3-5

Irresistibly Boxed Set 4-6

Hidden Alphas

Hidden Gabriel

Hidden Raphael

Hidden Michael

Hidden Dane

Hidden Rocco

Hidden Alphas Boxed Set

The Marshall Family Saga

Favorite Crush

Favorite Mistake

Favorite Sin

Favorite Scandal

The Collins Brothers

Sean

Daniel

Gerard

Liam

Eric

<u>Then if you also like</u>

<u>Science Fiction/Fantasy Romance</u>

Hidden Dragon Series

Call of the Dragon

Dawn of the Dragon

Escape of the Dragon (Coming Soon)

The Queen Gene

Whispers of a Throne

Storm of the Throne (coming soon)

Earthseekers Mission

Makeup May Change Your Life

The Zoastra Affair

Ancient Greek Heroes

Romancing Theseus

Mything the Throne

About the Author

USA Today Bestselling Author, Victoria Pinder grew up in Irish Catholic Boston then moved to Miami. Eventually, found that writing is her passion. She always wrote stories to entertain herself. Her parents are practical minded people demanding a job, but when she sat down to see what she enjoyed doing, writing became obvious.

Visit my website and download a free novel
www.victoriapinder.com
victoria@victoriapinder.com

Made in the USA
Monee, IL
29 July 2021

74569091R00152